AT FIRST MEET - SPECIAL EDITION

CARRIE ANN RYAN

AT FIRST MEET

A MONTGOMERY INK LEGACY NOVEL

By
Carrie Ann Ryan

At First Meet
A Montgomery Ink Legacy Novel
By: Carrie Ann Ryan
© 2022 Carrie Ann Ryan
eBook ISBN 978-1-63695-180-5
Paperback ISBN 978-1-63695-181-2

Cover Art by Sweet N Spicy Designs

"Count on Carrie Ann Ryan for emotional, sexy, character driven stories that capture your heart!" – Carly Phillips, NY Times bestselling author

"Carrie Ann Ryan's romances are my newest addiction! The emotion in her books captures me from the very beginning. The hope and healing hold me close until the end. These love stories will simply sweep you away." ~ NYT Bestselling Author Deveny Perry

"Carrie Ann Ryan writes the perfect balance of sweet and heat ensuring every story feeds the soul." - Audrey Carlan, #1 New York Times Bestselling Author

"Carrie Ann Ryan never fails to draw readers in with passion, raw sensuality, and characters that pop off the page. Any book by Carrie Ann is an absolute treat." – New York Times Bestselling Author J. Kenner

"Carrie Ann Ryan knows how to pull your heart-strings and make your pulse pound! Her wonderful Redwood Pack series will draw you in and keep you reading long into the night. I can't wait to see what comes next with the new generation, the Talons. Keep them coming, Carrie Ann!" –Lara Adrian, New York Times bestselling author of CRAVE THE NIGHT

AT FIRST MEET

NYT Bestselling Author Carrie Ann Ryan continues the Montgomery Ink Legacy series with an emotional, friends-to-lovers romance where second chances begin with a promise.

I fell in love with the wrong man and learned the hard way to ask for help.

I don't plan on falling again and have no intention of trying.

But when I get invited to a high-powered CEO retreat, I know I can't say no.

And I can't go alone.

When my frenemy, Nick, invites himself as my escort, I should walk away.

But there's no stopping the connection we've both ignored for far too long.

Only Nick's past is far darker than he lets the world know, and the shell he encased himself in is stronger than my own. And when the pain from my past comes back with a force, I'm afraid that walking away will be the only choice—even if it breaks us both.

Chapter 1

Lake

I MIGHT BE A MONTGOMERY, BUT I FELT LIKE A FRAUD. That is, until I looked around my office and remembered that a Montgomery could do anything. I might not have been born into this family, but I held the name, the connections, the love, and the will to succeed.

I smiled as I tapped on the keyboard, replying to another of the countless emails that had made their way to me.

My assistant and staff went through most of my emails before they even hit my inbox. Mostly because I worked way too many hours a day, had more than one job, more than one multimillion-dollar business, and somebody needed to organize my emails for me.

As somewhat of a control freak, it was odd to think that I even did that. Only here I was, looking through a list of emails that I should probably go through since they were forwarded to my private email address rather than the public one.

My intercom buzzed and I tapped it, smiling, even though Desiree couldn't see me.

"Yes, Desiree?" I asked, leaning back into my chair while rubbing my neck. I had been working nonstop for the past few hours, and as I looked at the clock, I knew exactly why she was buzzing.

"Don't skip lunch, or I'm going to have to deal with your parents. Please don't make me deal with your parents."

I held back a laugh because my parents weren't mean or overbearing. No. It was because my parents could love you to the point of feeling guilty when you weren't taking care of yourself. They would never blame Desiree for me forgetting to eat when I was focusing. But they would ensure that Desiree was eating.

"You only don't like it because if I forget lunch, it means you have also. Even though it's on our calendars."

Desiree walked in rather than finishing the conversation through the intercom.

I might have a corner office in Downtown Denver in one of the few large skyscrapers, but Desiree had her own office right next to mine. I wasn't going to put her in a tiny little seat where people would call her the dragon when they tried to get to me.

Okay, well, they still called her the dragon, and they had to get through her to get to me, but I wasn't going to force her to work out in the open where she couldn't have space to herself. So she had her own office. Her own office with a set of windows, a mini fridge, and more than one timer to remind us to eat lunch.

"I brought us salads because I was in the mood for it, but they're Mediterranean ones with tons of protein and chocolate chip cookies because it's not like we don't deserve it."

I rolled my eyes and gestured towards the seating area in my office. "Come on, the last time I ate dressing over my keyboard, the IT department growled at me. It's *my* building. If I want to drop a large drop of dressing and a crouton on my keyboard, I can."

Desiree rolled her eyes and sat down, handing me my food. I went and got us two sparkling waters, as well as a few napkins.

"Are we taking a true break, or are we having a working lunch?"

"You and I are both leaving early today, and when do we ever actually not talk about work during lunch?"

I winced. "Okay, you're right. Now let's talk."

"You have a meeting with Diana at one. Which is good because it was supposed to be noon, and then we would be meeting with her while eating salad."

"I could do that. With dressing running all down my chest."

"You do throw salad at yourself, don't you?"

I snorted and placed my napkin in my cleavage so I could protect my shirt. I might run multimillion-dollar companies, have a few million in the bank, and have graced a few magazine covers in my time, but I still ate sloppily. I couldn't help it. My mind was on a thousand different things, and I really was a dork.

Zach had always hated it. When I spilled on myself because I wasn't paying attention or the fact that I was just clumsy sometimes. He'd hated it so much, that was the first time he—

I cut myself off, ignoring the way my palms went clammy, and reminded myself that it didn't matter if Zach hated that I sometimes spilled on myself like a dork or a toddler. It wasn't his problem. He was gone, and he wasn't going to come back.

I was safe.

I sucked in a breath, chugged down half my water, then nearly choked because I forgot it was sparkling.

Desiree gave me a look, and I used my spare napkin to wipe my face and continued listening to what the rest of our day would be like.

Desiree didn't know. I think she had suspicions, but she didn't *know*. Most people didn't.

My parents and my siblings did because, despite myself, I couldn't keep secrets from them. I had tried, and I had actually succeeded to some extent. Then I broken down and needed my mother. I needed my mom. She had been there without a second thought. She hadn't blamed me for my mistakes. Nobody had. The only thing I had to do was hold my dad back from beating the shit out of Zach. That wouldn't have helped anything. I needed to hold back my cousin, Leif, as well.

I had gone to Leif when everything had happened, things I didn't even want to think about, but it hadn't been him who I'd told first.

It had been Nick.

I let out a breath and quickly continued to eat, listening to Desiree and taking mental notes as she spoke because I wasn't about to let my mind go down that path again.

It had been three months since I walked away from Zach after he had hit me the final time.

After the man that I had loved, the man that I had thought was my world, had wrapped his hands around my neck and threatened to kill me.

It had been three months since I started therapy—nearly every day for a month—and then twice a week after that just to get it out because my family hadn't allowed for anything else.

And while I hated them three months ago for forcing me to do it, I was grateful.

I was not yet whole, I was not happy or healthy or ready for the future. But I was healing.

Three months since the last time Zach told me that I was ugly. That I was fat. That I needed to lose part of myself in order to be with him.

Three months since I allowed part of myself to go into a secret place, to forget that person ever existed.

Three months since he had laid his hands on me. Three months since I allowed him to do so.

Then I was okay.

I worked in a high-powered profession and did what I needed to do to survive.

"Lake? What's wrong?" Desiree asked. She set down her fork, her meal forgotten just like mine, and I swallowed hard, grateful I wasn't crying.

I was so tired of crying.

"Sorry, I'm just thinking."

"Do you want to tell me about what?"

Desiree wasn't really my friend. We were close, but we didn't hang out outside of work. Mostly because she had four kids and a loving wife and had a life of her own. We weren't people who did much outside of our jobs, and I knew she was grateful for that. She needed time away from my demands and my busy schedule. While I tried to be the best boss, I had a lot of things on my plate, and that meant things needed to be done my way.

So she had seen the shadow I had slowly become when I hadn't been aware of it.

But I was no longer that woman. I wasn't the woman she had met when I had hired her, nor was I the woman of three months ago.

I knew three months wasn't long enough to feel whole. But I was doing better.

And if I kept telling myself that, it would make it true.

"Sorry, my brain keeps going in too many weird directions today. Personal things. I promise, I'm ready to talk with Diana, though. I'm excited about that project."

Desiree studied my face before she thankfully let it go. "I'm excited too. I know New Orleans has all the vampire places for a good reason, but honestly, Denver needs one, too."

I laughed, finishing my lunch as we spoke.

"You're right. I mean yes, there's more sunlight here than in New Orleans theoretically, but you know we have nighttime too. The vampires could roam in the night."

"And there could be daywalkers. And we know that I am a huge Twilight fan so we're just going to let it be known that I would be okay if sparkly vampires walked among us."

"As long as Jasper does, I'm fine," I purred, and Desiree burst out laughing, just like I wanted.

"I'm team Charlie all the way."

"Okay, I can get behind that," I laughed. "Seriously though, with all these woods and mountainous areas, there could be vampires living out there, or even downtown. And now there'll be a vampire café for them."

"We should add that to some of the media," Desiree said.

"I'm sure Diana has a whole idea for it," I said with a laugh, and we cleaned up the remnants of our lunch. I went back to my desk and brought up Diana's file.

Diana was a hardworking single mom of two young boys who used to own a small café in Seattle when she was in her twenties. That's when she met her husband, and the two of them worked on it together until he was killed in a freak train accident. The city had given her a small stipend, but not enough for the locale, and between that and the memories, Diana moved to Denver to start fresh. She currently worked for somebody else at another café, and the former owner was happy to help out because they wouldn't be competing with one another. Still, Diana was ready for something niche, something that would make her sons laugh and fit into a certain demographic.

Namely mine and my friends' demographic.

When Diana walked in, I smiled and got up, holding my hand out.

"I'm so glad that you're here. Let's talk."

"I can't believe you chose my proposal," Diana blurted. "Sorry. I know that's a weird thing to say right off the bat, but thank you, Ms. Montgomery."

"Please, call me Lake. And I chose your proposal because I like what you have planned, and you have an idea that has merit. And to be selfish, I want to go to your café."

"Just wait. I am so excited for the drinks and the food we're going to have, and we're not going to go too cheesy. I promise no random men with widow's peaks and overly white chompers that fall out while they're speaking with lisps."

"Oh, I've seen your proposal. I know exactly what you want to do."

We sat down and talked about cheese plates and

blood bags and other fun items that would go with the vampire club.

It wasn't going to be a dance hall. It wasn't going to be all about sex and drugs and everything that some might think a vampire café should be. This was going to be a wonderful afternoon and dinner place, to eat, have a drink, and listen to some open mic nights or other book club events. It was going to be fun. And that's what Diana wanted.

And that's what I wanted.

And that's what my job was.

"I'd love to know exactly how you got into this. You're so young. And here you are, helping out other women. I love it."

I was used to this question, so I answered it quickly. "I graduated from high school early, and while I was in college, I worked with a professor, and somehow I was lucky enough to invent some tech that did really well."

It wasn't the most detailed version of my life, but it was part of it.

"Well enough that I didn't have to focus too much on where I wanted to go after that, so I made sure I got my master's in business, and I now want to use what I've learned to help others. Others like you. I want to help women and those in need to finance what they want to do. Part of my business is owning our tech company and working towards the future, and the other part is going to the future in a different way. I want to make sure that small businesses can get off the ground without the huge worry that they can compete in a man's world. Because despite however far we've gone, we're not there yet. So I want to help you. Women-owned businesses need to be out there. They need to be at the forefront. We want single moms not to have to choose between working for themselves and ignoring their children and working for someone else and not paving the road for their children in the first place. So I'm going to help you. And I get a vampire café at the end of it."

Diana wiped tears away. I hadn't meant for her to cry.

This was my job—to make sure that I paid it forward. I made sure that others had the chance I was given.

By the time Diana left, I was smiling and I knew that I'd made the right decision accepting her proposal. There were a few more proposals I had to go through, as well as my own tech business to do. But I was doing well. I also happened to own a stake in the next generation of Montgomery Ink Tattoos with Montgomery Ink Legacy, so I wanted to stop by there later and meet up with my family.

I worked enough hours, had enough jobs that I

didn't have to worry about going home to an empty house.

Because at least *he* wouldn't be there.

I shuddered, and as I closed the door, the delivery man dropped a ream of paper. It echoed in the building and I froze, sweat sliding down my back as a metallic taste slid over my tongue. My hands shook, and I was grateful no one could see me. I gently closed the door as I fought to suck in breaths. But nothing would come. My airways closed, and I staggered over to the bar area and poured myself a glass of water from the pitcher, sloshing some over the rim as I forced myself to drink, to breathe.

Close your eyes, Lake.

Count to ten.

One.

Two.

Three.

I didn't even have to get to ten before I could breathe.

That wasn't bad, that time. I was getting better.

But I texted my therapist and told her about it anyway. We would talk about it in the morning for my next session, and I would find a way to get over it.

Because I had to.

I couldn't help others if I couldn't help myself. So I needed to get over it.

There was a knock at the door, and I quickly looked in the mirror, making sure I looked presentable.

I looked fine. Not sweaty or pale or as if I just had another panic attack for no reason. I looked like Lake Montgomery, kick-ass CEO who could do no wrong.

And that's what the world needed to see.

"Come in," I called as Desiree walked in.

Her eyes were wide as she handed me an envelope.

"What is it?"

"I think I have an idea, but I need you to open it."

I frowned, but I pulled the gold envelope from her hand and nearly dropped it.

"*Elite*? Wait, what day is it?"

"It's the day you think it is," Desiree answered.

I quickly opened the envelope. Odd that they would send letters like this rather than emails or phone calls.

Because I knew what day it was and exactly what this should be.

Lake Montgomery, we invite you to the Elite 40 Under 40 retreat of the year. You are our 40 Under 40. CEOs who have set an example for the world and are our future.

RSVP.

There was more information, but I just stared at her.

"I can't, seriously? How is that even possible?"

"You know how that's possible. You are the best boss ever and are Elite."

"I just can't believe they picked me. I mean, I do kick ass. We kick ass," I emphasized as I looked between us both, and Desiree beamed.

"Well, you kick ass, and I know you're thinking about the fact that there's only ever been a handful of women invited."

"Bingo," I mouthed. "There's probably what, one or two women each year for how many years now? I can't believe I'm one of them. I can't believe I just said that as if that's a good thing," I growled.

"It is a good thing. You can't say no to this. You have to go."

I nodded tightly. "I know I do. It's good for the company. It's good for our future. It's good for the women that I can help. And hell, I guess it's good for me."

Desiree grinned, talking a mile a minute, as I looked down at the invitation again and looked at what I had missed the first go-around.

Lake Montgomery plus one.

As in, I needed to bring someone with me.

And I couldn't go by myself, not as a woman, to a male-oriented event. And not as a woman who most recently hid from the world because she hadn't been able to see the monster beneath.

And I had no one to take. No one because I wanted no one.

I had made the wrong choice before, and I wasn't going to do it again.

But I couldn't go alone. Not to something like this.

And once again, I felt like a fraud.

Because a Montgomery would know what to do.

Chapter 2

Nick

"HEY, NICK, DO YOU WANT COFFEE? I'M CRAVING something sweet. And I need the boost."

I nodded and looked over at my fellow tattoo artist, Leo. "Coffee sounds good."

"What do you want? The usual? Or something spicy?"

I shuddered and glared over at Leo. "Is spicy coffee a thing? Is this what the kids are doing these days?"

Sebastian, my co-owner of Montgomery Ink Legacy and friend, snorted. "I don't think the kids these days are making spicy coffee. I'm just imagining some form of hot sauce in coffee just to see if they can handle it."

I shuddered. "I don't think that's for me."

"Actually, you can put cayenne pepper in coffee. I've had Mexican mocha coffee, and a Moroccan spiced coffee that's pretty decent," Brooke, my friend's girl said as she looked over a stack of papers she was grading. She was here visiting Leif, my fellow co-owner, best friend, and blood brother.

"Well, now I want to try all of that," Leo said. "But I don't think we're going to get it at the café at the corner."

Sebastian looked down at his phone. "This says you can make it with a rich blend of coffee, cream, cinnamon, nutmeg, and cayenne pepper."

Scowling, my stomach rumbled. "Damn it. Now I want to try it. And we're not going to find it at that place."

"I bet Hailey would have it at Taboo," Brooke added helpfully.

Liam walked in and kissed the top of her head. "We need her to franchise as well. That way she can put in a shop next to us. I got spoiled downtown."

I frowned, wrote down a few notes. "I wonder why she hasn't franchised. Or your aunt and uncle down in Colorado Springs who have that bakery. They do coffee too, right?"

"Some, but they don't go into the specialties as much as Taboo does. And I think Hailey had her hands full with the downtown branch. I don't think they need to put it in a strip mall on the other side of town."

"Stop saying strip mall like it's a bad thing," Brooke said. "You guys are killing it here. I'm very proud."

I rolled my eyes, even though I was pleased that we were doing well.

Putting my life savings into this venture had been scary, even though I had worked my ass off to get here. I had trained with the best—Leif's parents and family members down at Montgomery Ink in Denver and other friends down in New Orleans. I had learned my craft, saved money and gone into owning Montgomery Ink Legacy with Leif Montgomery, Sebastian Montgomery, and Lake Montgomery.

Lake wasn't even a tattoo artist but a friend of all of ours, even if we growled at each other more than not. She had wanted to do something with the obscene amount of money she made at a young age, and apparently we were her charity case. That was fine with me because I got to do what I wanted, thanks to her. Though I didn't have to ask her, I didn't have to thank her often. Or ever, if I had any say in it.

"Really though, what kind of coffee do you want?" Leo asked.

Montgomery Ink Legacy, or MIL for short, might have been owned and operated by three tattoo artists and Lake, but Sebastian was still under twenty years old, in college, and going to be a father soon, which was insane to me. He was here to learn, had some of his own clients, but hadn't bought in fully like we had. Lake helped with the books but worked with her own multimillion-dollar company and was rarely here. Thankfully. Not that I would say that to her.

Mostly because that was my problem and not hers, and I wasn't in the mood to deal with it.

So Leif and I did most of the client work, and I was fine with that. We had hired three other tattoo artists to work with us.

Tristan, Taryn, and Leo. The three of them worked together well and were a crew of their own. All three were also experienced and licensed piercers, so we ran the gambit here at MIL.

Leo was a friend, and since he was getting me coffee, he was my best friend.

"Something iced, cream and sugar. I'm not in the mood for just black coffee."

"Have enough hair on your chest?" Sebastian asked, poring over his business books. At least, I thought it was a business class. I wasn't sure since Sebastian was taking more credit hours than I thought reasonable and helping his pregnant girlfriend or fiancée through her initial stages of pregnancy. It was a little too much for him, but he was kicking ass, and I was always there if he needed me.

"Yes, I do. There are no complaints."

"He says that, and yet he hasn't introduced me to a single girlfriend," Brooke teased.

I glared at the woman, even though I liked her. "Because as soon as I introduce you or any of the other women to her, it's going to be a thing. And I don't need it to be a thing. I'm just fine with my relationships as they are."

"Imaginary, or just your left hand?" Sebastian asked.

Leo barked out a laugh, the others joining as I just shook my head, my lips twitching.

"It's my right, thank you very much. I can be ambidextrous with more than just tattoos."

"I still can't believe you can do both." Brooke blushed as everyone laughed.

Leif put his hands over his face. "Babe. Really?"

"I meant tattooing. Not fucking your fist."

We all froze for an instant, blinking at that phrase coming from her mouth, though Leif didn't sound surprised.

Damn, Brooke was all full of surprises; no wonder I liked her.

"That's an image I'm going to carry with me until

the end of my days," Leo said with a sigh. "And on that note, I got everyone's coffee orders. I'll be back. But I'm not going to get Taboo's coffee like I want."

"I guess we can all go work on her to start franchising so we can have Taboo next door. I'm sure she'll do it just for us," Sebastian said.

"Exactly. We won't have to wait for long," Leif said with a laugh.

"Now that we have that out of our systems, I'm headed out," Brooke said as she stood up, rubbing her back.

"Are you okay?" Leif asked, concern in his tone.

She smiled up at him, and I tried not to feel jealous. I didn't want Brooke, I liked her, but it wasn't like that.

The way that she looked at Leif like he was the center of her universe? I don't know. It might have been nice to have that. I never had, not even as a kid. I didn't think I was going to have something like that ever. But I didn't complain. I had a good life. Had my friends, this shop. I didn't need much else.

And that wasn't a lie at all.

"I'm fine. I just slept at an odd angle all night."

I whistled under my teeth along with Sebastian, and Brooke narrowed her gaze. "Because Luke had a nightmare, and he ended up sleeping between us all night. Get your head out of the gutter. Both of you.

You're about to be a dad, Sebastian. Just know it's going to happen to you too. Late night feedings, diaper explosions, and even when they get older, they're going to come to you and scare the hell out of you. How, you ask? Well, what they're going to do is they don't want to wake you up completely. They don't want to startle you by touching your face or jostling you awake or even saying your name. Instead they're just going to stand beside your bed, waiting quietly. Staring without blinking. Until even within your dream you feel a presence there. Knowing. Waiting and watching. You open your eyes in the dark, only the moonlight sliding through the cracks in the blinds, illuminating your son's pale face with wide unblinking eyes.

"And as you try not to scream, not to scare your son or the man sleeping next to you, all you do is let out a chirping noise. One that startles Leif awake, going 'What, what,' and flopping around on the bed as if he were an injured seal. And then your son cries and is so sorry that he startled you, but all you can hear is your heart in your ears and bile on your tongue because you just thought that the kid from *The Grudge* is at the side of your bed, making that weird guttural throat sound. That is your future. And you're going to love it."

I sat there as the others laughed, my eyes wide. "That was very descriptive. And a little scary."

"A whole lot scary. The first time he did it to me, I thought there was an actual monster in the room. Instead, it's just our kid."

The two of them looked at each other and smiled, and I swallowed hard.

Their kid. They hadn't even been together a year yet, weren't married, but Luke was *their* kid.

I wasn't jealous, but damn I was happy for Leif. He deserved this. So did Brooke.

"For real, though, I'm leaving. I have a class this afternoon, and then tomorrow is all-day seminars. Are you good picking up Luke since May has an appointment?"

"I'm on it. We've got this."

They kissed softly, and a little too long for my taste, until finally Sebastian cleared his throat.

"Our next appointments come in soon. I don't know if you guys want to be making out in front of them."

Leif didn't even bother to look at us. Instead, he flipped us off, and Brooke laughed, blushing slightly as she waved and said her goodbyes.

"I need to head out too. I promised Marley I would meet her for lunch between classes. I have a night class tonight, then labs all day tomorrow."

"Sounds good. You have clients on Friday, right?" Leif asked.

Technically, Sebastian was an apprentice. He needed more time to learn and was going to business school so he could help out and we could grow as a company. While MIL was a subsidiary of the original Montgomery Ink, just like Montgomery Ink Too was down in Colorado Springs, we were the heavy investors. This was our company. And we didn't want it to fail.

I had all the hope and trust and faith in my partners, in the Montgomery family.

After all, they had practically raised me. They had been there when nobody else had, so I wasn't about to not believe in what they could do.

"Yep. You'll be there too, right? To hover over me to make sure I don't fuck up?" Sebastian was teasing, but I heard the worry in his tone.

It was daunting and exhilarating, and I knew that Sebastian was feeling everything that we had when we had first started.

Of course, we hadn't had impending fatherhood and marriage on our shoulders like he did.

"We'll be here. Watching over you like mother hens, don't worry," Leif teased, and I snorted, narrowing my eyes at the sketch in front of me.

It wasn't right yet, and I had two more versions to show my client.

She wanted a full side piece of broken and growing

branches, to show where she had been, and where she wanted to go.

She wanted it in grayscale. I didn't blame her. She had had a full-color tattoo about a decade ago from another artist, and the color had faded to almost nothing in a couple of years, her skin not reacting in the way that most other skin did. The outline had also blown out, and she had been hesitant for another tattoo for a while.

We had done a smaller tattoo on her hip in the meantime, just to see if she could handle another one, and it had worked out.

So we didn't know what had happened, other than we needed to be careful, and she wasn't going full color. I didn't mind, but that meant that I had to be careful with my shading, and have the drawing and sketch work with what I wanted, to enhance the draw-ing, rather than just have something in black and white that didn't make much sense.

"I have our coffees. No cayenne pepper," Leo said as he came in, the coffees already sweating in his hands.

It was humid outside, which was a rare gift to most of Colorado.

Colorado was dry as hell and always led to dehy-dration and altitude sickness for people who hadn't lived here before. But the fact that we had humidity right now was weird. I didn't like it, and never wanted to ever visit a place that was high humidity. For instance, Florida was never going to be on my bucket list, even though I knew that our friends all wanted to go down to EPCOT one year and eat and drink our way around the world. That sounded fun, but doing so in Satan's hellhole of humidity didn't.

"Thanks, I'm headed out," Sebastian said, and Leo nodded.

"Have fun. Learn all the things."

"I'm trying."

Sebastian said his goodbyes as Leif leaned back in his chair and stared at his phone.

"What is it?" I asked.

"Lake was going to stop by, but just texted to say that she had another meeting. I hate that she's working herself too hard."

Leo looked between us and kept silent.

Everyone in this room knew part of what had happened to Lake. It wasn't like we could hide it since we were all friends and family.

But I had been the one to first see her.

I had been watching Luke for the night, staying at Brooke's place while Brooke and Leif went out for a date. I liked the kid, and I hadn't minded staying.

And I don't know, maybe part of me had wanted to be there, knowing that Lake lived next door.

Because part of me had known something was wrong. I didn't know what it was, and I should have known.

I should have thought about more than just the fact that asshole Zach had given me the creeps.

I had told myself I needed to get over my overprotectiveness, that Lake wasn't my sister, was only my friend, and even then, we fought more than we actually liked each other.

But I had been the one that she had asked for help. Help.

One word, four letters, something I hadn't even known she knew.

Because Lake Montgomery did not ask for help. She had become a Montgomery later in her life and had worked her ass off to prove that she was worthy of becoming part of that family.

Which in my head was fucking ridiculous because she didn't need to work at all to become a Montgomery. That family loved all of their people, even ones that sometimes fucked up, because no matter what, they were family, and they took care of each other. There was no sniping or growling beyond the usual. They cared for one another. There was no jealousy or trying to outdo one another. The Montgomerys took care of their own.

And somehow, along the way, I had become one of

their own too. Because their own weren't just those with the Montgomery iris tattoo—a flowered circle with their family crest that each member of the family got tattooed on their bodies because they wanted to, not because they had to.

So I didn't know why Lake had worked so hard to try to fit in with a family that loved her beyond all measure.

But maybe I didn't know Lake. All I knew was that we growled at each other and fought no matter what we did. We were co-owners of this damn place and always yelled at one another.

And I wasn't going to dive too deep into the why of that.

Yet I had been the one standing there, the one watching her as she put her hands to her neck; and the bruises etched on her skin would forever haunt my dreams.

Because she had tried to cover them up. So many different kinds of makeup all blended together, but I could still see.

That bastard had wrapped his hands around her throat and tried to kill her.

Though the cops didn't believe that.

They let her put a restraining order on him, but that was it. Zach was still out there, not in jail because apparently those bruises only meant that he might have hurt her once. Because Lake hadn't gone to the authorities the other times he had hit her or emotionally put her into a cage and treated her like shit, so when she began to wear sweatshirts with baggy pants and her hair up in a bun instead of done to the nines like she always did, it wasn't worth putting the man in jail.

Then again, I knew all too well what happened when somebody broke your spirit, but not the law.

There was only so much you could do, so Zach was out there, but so was Lake.

And she wasn't here again today.

I didn't want to be the selfish asshole who thought it was because of me.

But she didn't see me anymore.

In the three months since that day, I had only seen her a handful of times.

The others saw her, and I knew she came into work on the days that I wasn't here. And I didn't know if it was on purpose or not.

But Lake Montgomery seemed to be avoiding me. It was the only thing that made sense.

And I fucking hated it.

I didn't know why I hated it so much.

"She'll be here tomorrow, though," Leif added, looking down at his phone.

On my day off. Not that I said that out loud.

"Whatever," I growled, going back to my sketch.

The look that the other two shared didn't escape my notice, but I ignored it.

Just like I ignored the text from the unknown number next to me, as my phone buzzed once again.

I didn't want to deal with that right then, I didn't want to deal with anything.

The world kept moving on around me, and I was standing still.

Maybe I needed to not worry about everything I couldn't control.

Chapter 3

Lake

"I'M SAD THAT MARLEY CAN'T BE HERE," BROOKE SAID as she set the cheeseboard on the coffee table.

I nodded, setting the two bottles of wine and the glasses next to them. My hands ached from holding all of that at once, but I hadn't been in the mood to make more than one trip.

I was using my former waitressing skills for a purpose.

"She's with her parents tonight." May came forward and set down the spinach dip in a bread bowl next to the cheeseboard. "You would think that she wasn't an adult or something with the way that they treat her."

I nodded, my heart twisting for the young woman who was facing a new life and dealing with a family that didn't understand her.

"She's an adult, just like Sebastian is. Yes, they're a little young for having kids—at least that would be too young for me. What do I know? It's their lives. They're adults. They're making their decisions. I'm not sure what her parents could possibly do."

Brooke shook her head as she poured us each a glass of wine. "I deal with students her age every day. There's this odd dichotomy of becoming an adult and still relying on your parents for certain things. Marley isn't one that constantly goes back to her parents for affection or needs or money or anything like that. She and Sebastian are each working to pay for half of their college, while their parents pay for the other half. It's the deal that they made. And I like that deal. It's what I might do for Luke."

I smiled, thinking of Luke, who was now out with Leif and the crew tonight for a guys' evening.

"Marley and Sebastian both have great heads on their shoulders, and they're not going to do this alone. And honestly, I'm kind of excited for a new baby." Brooke smiled, and May and I met gazes, grinning.

"Are you and Leif planning on something that I

should know about?" I asked, fluttering my eyelashes. "Are you going to make me an auntie again?"

Technically, Leif and I were cousins. My father and Leif's father were Montgomerys, but with our generation, it was just easier to call us all siblings or aunts and uncles and other things. Leif and I had been raised practically as siblings, considering we were closer in age than the others. I didn't really think about the fact that once he and Brooke got married, that Luke would be my cousin once removed, or second cousin. I wasn't quite sure how that worked. In my mind, he would be my nephew. Especially considering the fact that Brooke and I were like sisters these days. My best friend. And I was grateful she was in my life.

"Oh no. We need some time. We're still pretty new in this whole relationship thing. Even if it feels like we've been together forever."

"I kind of agree, though. It'll be nice for a new baby. For the next generation to start. I know my parents are sort of getting excited about becoming great-aunts and uncles."

"Not grandparents?" May asked, grinning, and I laughed outright.

"My siblings are a little too young for that."

The girls didn't mention the fact that I was not too young to be a parent. But I wasn't anywhere near ready for that. I thought I had found the person I could be with. The person that would make everything better. That would be my happy ever after. But I was wrong. Oh so wrong. Zach was 'nothing like what I needed in life. And I wasn't ready to take that chance again. I was pretty sure I was never going to take that chance again.

I didn't need to think about it.

"Anyway," Brooke said. "I'm glad we're doing this girls' night. We haven't had a lot of time to just hang out."

"We do okay," I countered. "We just had a dinner the other day."

"Yes, but it still doesn't feel like enough most of the time. I like that we hang out as much as we do. And that today is just about us." She smiled as she said it, and I smiled right back.

"It is nice that tonight's about us. Plus, I didn't have to cook dinner since you did all the cooking today."

I looked over at May, who blushed.

"Luke helped. He's getting really good at this whole cooking thing."

"Well, I'm glad you're teaching him, because I get to reap the benefits," Brooke said with a laugh.

"Now, why don't you tell us this news?" Brooke said as she sipped her wine.

I blinked, before I grinned. "You're right. I forgot that I was going to mention this one thing."

Great, I thought.

"Well, I was officially nominated and awarded top forty CEOs under forty in the country with *Elite*."

The girls paused, then their eyes brightened as each let out a high-pitched squeal and jumped to their feet.

"Oh my God. That's amazing."

I blushed and looked down at my empty wine glass. "I feel like a fraud."

"Excuse me?" May asked. "Don't you dare feel like a fraud, lady."

"I can't help it. All of those CEOs are in big business. Yes, my company does great work, and the subsidiary company that helps other businesses does even better work. But I don't really think of myself as a CEO."

"Okay, we have a lot to unpack in those statements. First," Brooke began, "you are a damn CEO. You run a multimillion-dollar company. You travel all over the world with your tech and business. Your coding for that tech has won awards. You have countless patents under your belt and even more underneath the company's belt.

"Not to mention you've helped dozens of women-owned companies succeed. You've put down micro-loans and capital to make that happen. You've allowed other companies to help those companies by teaching them about those loans. You have done so much good, and you're only just beginning. You're amazing. So why do you think you don't belong?"

I scrunched my face. "I don't like it when you put it all out like that. It makes me sound like I've done a lot more than I have."

"You have done a lot. You'll do even more. I'm so proud to call you my friend. Top forty under forty? Amazing."

"I don't know, I always found it a little ageist that they even have that. Like as soon as I hit forty I'm no longer good enough?"

"That's a whole other thing." May shook her head. "I mean, it's nice to see the next generations working up towards things. And it's not like the men in their late forties, fifties, sixties, and seventies are letting go of power anytime soon," May singsonged.

I snorted, shook my head. "Okay. You're right. Damn you. But still, it's amazing, isn't it? And crazy."

"So, what does this honor mean?"

"It means I get to go to their retreat. Which is insane. And there's only two women going. Two women out of the top forty. And I'm one of them."

Brooke blinked. "I can't say that I'm surprised considering my job in academia."

I heard the wryness in her tone, and considering everything Brooke had gone through with her PhD in physics and now in some of the top research, I didn't blame her.

"That's not great optics," May said softly.

"Not even a little. So it's not like I can turn it down. I have issues with it, issues with the magazine in charge of it, and some of the connections you get through it, but I can't turn it down. Because I am one of the two women awarded."

"What does it entail?" Brooke asked.

"It begins with a retreat. I get to fly out to a luxury hotel, go through some classes, some bonding techniques, and it's all about the networking. People will get to know my company and my name. It will do great things for the company. Meaning I can put more money into other projects and help others. And I'm working towards that patient advocacy group. With the connections I can make, especially with this one company, I can do so much good."

"Plus, you earned this. You deserve some recognition," May added.

"Maybe. Sometimes I would rather just keep my head down to work. However, there's a problem."

"What's the problem?" Brooke asked.

"Everybody there is bringing their spouse. Or their significant other. Or something like that. There're no children going to this, but you bring your person. They network as well. It's a see-and-be-seen retreat. It's this whole other level that I don't want to be part of, but it's not like I can avoid."

Brooke winced. "The faculty dinners have that. I bring Leif and people just stare at him."

I snorted, I couldn't help it. Just thinking about the fact that my tattooed and bearded cousin would be entrenched in a room with academics in tweed suits made me laugh.

Brooke narrowed her eyes. "I know what you're thinking. There are no tweed suits to be seen."

I threw my head back and laughed, surprised I could even do so.

"Oh come on. How the hell did you know I was thinking tweed?"

"Because you think of a professor of physics, and you think of tweed. Okay, Dr. Simmons might wear tweed, but not all the time. And not to faculty dinners. And you know that Leif can clean up good."

May hummed under her breath. "Yes, he can."

Brooke narrowed her gaze at her nanny, before she snorted. "I'll forever be grateful that your blind date with Leif didn't work out."

"I'm forever grateful that you don't mind the fact that I dated your boyfriend first."

The two laughed, and I just shook my head, wincing. I had been the one to set up May on that date with Leif. It hadn't worked out for them, though in the end it had been great for Brooke. Of course, my date had been with Zach that night. And that had been the beginning of the end, even if I hadn't realized it in time.

If only I had.

"So what are you going to do?" May asked after we calmed down.

"Go alone, I guess. I mean, why should I have to bring a date to this? This is about me. My accomplishments. Me bringing a man to the event just to save face seems like I'm taking a few steps back, don't you think?"

"If you felt that you had to take somebody like that, maybe, but it's on them. What they think doesn't matter. Would you want to bring a friend with you so you're not there alone? That's another thing."

"Maybe." And Brooke was right about that. I didn't want to go alone, but it wasn't like I could bring my admin with me. Or even a cousin. No, if I brought a family member, it would be like bringing my cousin to prom. I didn't need to deal with that. But I also wasn't sure if I wanted to go alone. But I was good about being alone. I needed to be.

I just didn't like this feeling that I was doing something wrong.

We thankfully changed the subject to Luke, a

subject that I adored, and we finished our dinner, before I had to head back home.

"I have a stack of papers to read and proposals to go through, so I'm going to walk across the lawn to my house. But thank you for dinner."

"Thank you for coming. And we'll figure out what to do for your retreat. I'm so damn proud of you." Brooke kissed my cheek, then May kissed the other, and I laughed before I said my goodbyes.

I walked across the lawn, grateful that Brooke still lived there, but I knew she wouldn't for long. Leif had a bigger house, and they'd be moving in soon. They were just waiting for the final paperwork to go through.

It would be weird to think that I wouldn't have her next door any longer, even though I hadn't known Brooke for too long. Not even a year, and yet everything had changed.

The porch light was on, so I saw the shadow well ahead of time.

I held back a scream as I looked down at the bouquet of dead flowers on my porch.

It looked as if it had hit a window.

The bouquet lay there, the rose petals strewn about the porch.

But that was the problem. Because someone had torn those petals. The rose petals had been torn from the stalks, their thorns still evident on the stems.

I knew what this was. A threat. It had to be.

Because nobody else would be leaving me flowers.

I quickly took a few photos, and then called my contact with the police.

I knew what they would say before they even said it, but it wasn't like I could not call them.

"Go back to Brooke's house. We'll send somebody by."

I sighed. "I want to go inside. I just want to go home. I'm tired of this."

"Zach is out of town," he said, and I swallowed hard, my throat constricting. "He's not here. This wasn't him, Lake, but he could have hired someone, or something else. This could be kids for all we know. A prank. We'll send someone out."

"I'll be fine. But I guess tonight's going to be a long night."

"Go to Brooke's. We'll be there soon."

I hung up, and I stood there, and though I knew nobody was watching me, I still shivered before I headed back to Brooke's, and tried to think of what exactly I would say, knowing I couldn't lie.

I couldn't keep secrets, not anymore.

But I just wanted this to be over.

And I knew it wouldn't be. Possibly ever.

Because Zach hadn't gone to jail. There was a restraining order against him because he had hurt me, but the charges were dropped because he had friends in high places. Because his parents were judges, his sister and brother lawyers. Even his in-laws were lawyers. He had connections that I didn't. And he would hurt my company, and the startups and patient advocacy groups that I was working with. He had threatened all of that, so I had made sure he had gone away, but I couldn't do anything else. Not since this was his first offense, not since I knew he could hurt me again, even without laying his hands on me.

So there was nothing I could do except wait. And hope. And try to pretend everything was normal.

Even though I knew nothing was normal. And it would never be again.

Chapter 4

Nick

I watched as Luke ran from Sebastian to Leo, and then Leif, and shook my head, sitting back in my seat before I took a sip of my beer. It was warm so I set it aside, figuring I wouldn't finish it.

"Not in the mood?" Noah asked, and I looked over at Leif's cousin and shook my head.

"No, I have to drive later, and I wasn't even sure I wanted a beer. I think I just got it because I wasn't in the mood for a Coke."

"Yeah, I have more fun when we're at the bowling alley when we're just hanging out like this. With Luke around, though, I don't want to be the idiot who drinks too much."

I narrowed my gaze. "Are you even old enough to drink, Noah Montgomery Gallagher?" I asked, my voice a low growl.

Noah just grinned. "I'm as old as I need to be, thank you very much."

I took that as a no, then looked down at the root beer in Noah's hands. He winked at me, and I rolled my eyes.

The Montgomerys were rule followers, at least somewhat. Sure they might have a drink or two out in a field after a football game or steal a quick sip when their parents weren't looking like many normal teenagers did, but they didn't have fake IDs, and they didn't get drunk at a bowling alley when we were here with Leif's soon-to-be kid.

I wasn't a huge bowling fan, and frankly, I wasn't good at it, but if this was what Luke wanted to do, this is what we did.

Apparently, the five-year-old ruled us all, and we just went with it. I didn't mind. The kid was cute as hell, and he made Leif smile. My best friend needed to smile. He deserved everything in the world, and I was glad that he was getting it. Brooke was good for him. I was just annoyed that it had taken him this long to realize it.

"Okay, Noah, you're up," Leif said, and Noah got up from his seat and passed by Leif, who had Luke on his shoulders, spinning the kid around as they left the bowling lane.

I looked down at my shoes and cringed. I looked like a damn clown with my size thirteen feet, but it could have been worse. I could own these shoes. Become a professional bowler.

"When did we become bowlers?" I asked.

"Bowling is fun, Uncle Nick," Luke said as he grinned at me.

I met Leif's gaze and smiled. I liked being Uncle Nick. I didn't have any siblings, but I had been friends with Leif since we were teens. We had gone to high school and college together, and now owned a business together. I had stayed over at the Montgomerys' house more than my own some weeks in high school when things had gotten too rough. Leif's parents had been at my graduation cheering for me right along with their kid, even though they had been going through tough times of their own. My mom hadn't even bothered to show up.

I knew later it was because she'd had another episode and had apologized, but I still hated the fact that she hadn't been there.

But Leif's family had. And now Leif was doing his

best to be the man in Luke's life, even though I knew he wouldn't replace Luke's birth dad.

"His next birthday party he wants a bowling theme, so we're practicing. He's not that bad at it."

"I'm not that bad at it," the kid parroted, and I grinned.

"Better than me. We don't even need the bumpers for you."

"There are bumpers? I should have gotten the bumpers," Sebastian said as he worked on his tablet.

He was finishing up his homework while he hung out; he hadn't even wanted to come out tonight. But the kid rarely had time to breathe between school, Marley, impending fatherhood, and working at the shop. But we had dragged him out here because he hadn't been out on his own for a night with the guys in too long. And him being around Luke would be good for him.

I had no idea how to be a dad or what it entailed, and we were all learning with Luke. And he came pre-done. He was already five. We didn't have to worry about diapers and midnight feedings and all of that. And we would be here when the kid hit his preteens, and gangly ages, then teenage years and college. We'd be here for all of it. So Luke would be the one that we learned from first.

And then we'd help figure out Sebastian's brood.

And I would be Uncle Nick. Something I didn't even realize I wanted. But I liked it.

"Strike!" Noah said as he pumped his fist in the air.

Luke cheered, scrambled off Leif's hip, and ran towards Noah.

Noah laughed, spun Luke around, and dragged him back to the area.

"You're up, Gatlin."

I shuddered, standing up. "Okay. But don't laugh."

"We would never laugh at you, Uncle Nick."

I ran my hands through Luke's hair and winked. "You might not because you're a bigger person. These guys? They're going to laugh."

"Because we're laughing with you, not at you," Leif said as he sat down and pulled Luke with him, so he was out of the way of the balls coming down the chute.

The girls were having an appetizer and wine party at Brooke's place while we were bowling. Not out partying or doing anything else that people would be doing at our age. But bowling.

I lined up my shot, swung back, and barely missed hitting the gutter.

Noah and Sebastian threw their heads back and laughed. Leif did a valiant job of not laughing as Luke frowned.

"No, Uncle Nick. You're throwing it at an angle.

You don't need to toss it down, so it makes that loud sound."

"Yes, Uncle Nick, listen," Noah teased, and I flipped him off.

Leif growled and put his hands over Luke's eyes. "Family establishment."

"Sorry," I grumbled, and actually was sorry about it. I had forgotten. We were so used to doing that at work and just with each other, I forgot that I was actually in a place where there were kids around. Luckily, I didn't think anyone had noticed, and there weren't many kids there tonight.

"It's okay. Mom said that was for adults. Not me."

"Good. And I guess you can tell her what Uncle Nick did. Because we don't keep secrets."

"Don't worry, I will."

I scowled and knew that Brooke wouldn't say anything, but she would be disappointed. And I hated when she was disappointed.

She and Lake had that perfect look of, not anger, but "I thought you could do better." And I hated it. Because I usually could do better.

Not that I cared too much about what they thought. I wasn't dating either one of them. They weren't my women. And yet, I felt like I was losing my damn mind.

I pulled out my phone and thought about who I

shouldn't be texting as Sebastian went up to the lane. Something was off with her. Something she didn't want to talk about. And I wanted to know what it was. Why the hell was she avoiding me?

Duh, you asshole. You know exactly why she's avoiding you. Because you were the one that saw.

Of course, she didn't want to see you.

I stuffed my phone back into my pocket and ignored it. I wasn't going to text her. I wasn't going to ask her how she was doing.

That would just lead to questions and awkward conversations. And that dissapointed look all over again.

We finished out the game and I lost, just like we knew I would. Even the kid had beat me by a good fifteen points. And he did it granny style.

I shook my head in disgust as I got back in my car, the guys ragging on me.

"Don't worry, Uncle Nick. I'll teach you before my party."

I grinned before rolling my eyes over his head at Leif.

I liked being called Uncle Nick all right, but hell, I could use a better refrain than getting last place out of a group of five. Including a five-year-old of all people.

I drove back home, knowing that I had an early morning. I had an appointment that would take all day

—a full back piece outline. We would work on the other steps in two or three more sessions, but tomorrow was the big day, and I had to go home early and not be hungover or exhausted.

I got home, got myself a water, then went to work out. Just a few sets on my weights, nothing too strenuous. Only, I knew that wasn't what I wanted to do.

I wanted to text Lake and ask her what the hell she was thinking. Why she wouldn't talk to me. But that wouldn't get anything done. She was far more stubborn than anyone else I knew. If I contacted her and asked her why the hell she wouldn't talk to me, she would say it was all in my head, which it probably was. And then she would continue not to in response.

I growled, finished my sets, then wiped the sweat off my chest before stomping to the bedroom. I needed to go to bed early.

Instead, I pulled out my phone and did what I told myself I wouldn't.

Me: *Are you coming in to work tomorrow? I got a piece I want to show you.*

Not totally a lie, but why the hell was I texting her after nine?

Three little dots popped up on Lake's name, and I swallowed hard, wondering why I was nervous that she was even texting me back.

At least she had read it, and was thinking about

texting me back. For all I knew she was just going to send a thumbs down emoji, or no text at all. And I would have to remain on read until the end of my days. It wasn't like we owned a business together or anything. Oh wait. We did. Why the hell was she avoiding me?

Why was I wringing myself up in knots for a friend? A coworker.

Lake: I *might. I have a few things to do. Plus I need to pack.*

I frowned.

Me: *What do you mean pack? Did I know you were going on a business thing?*

Lake traveled often for work, and I was proud of her for it. The fact that she was able to travel the world because of her job was pretty fucking awesome. It wasn't something I ever wanted to do, but she got to see things, experience them. Maybe one day I'd be able to do a couple of those things, but sure as hell not in first-class or at fancy hotels like she did.

Lake: *Can I just call you?*

I sat up, frowned, and wondered if she had ever asked me to do that before. She had never once asked me, right? We didn't talk on the phone. That wasn't who we were. But if she needed me, of course I would talk to her.

Me: *Of course.*

The phone lit up with her name right away and I swallowed hard, wondering if I should put on my shoes to go pick her up or something. Was she in trouble? Was it her fucking ex?

My hands fisted at my side, but I told myself it was okay.

I was just losing my damn mind.

"Lake? Are you okay?" I asked in rapid staccato as soon as I answered.

She let out a breath, and I groaned, wondering why the hell I was like this. "I'm sorry. I didn't mean to make you think I was in trouble or anything. I'm okay, Nick. Just stressed. I promise."

It wasn't disappointment in her tone, but was it *shame*? Fuck. Because there was no way that she needed to feel shame. She had done nothing wrong, but no matter what I said, she was never going to believe me.

And that wasn't on her or me, but on that asshole ex.

"I've had a long day, sorry. Plus, we don't talk, sweet cakes. You know that."

I heard the little growl over the line and smiled.

"I hate that you sometimes call me random food items. I'm not your sweet cake. Your cupcake. Your butter cake. I'm not cake."

"What about donut? Like a glazed donut? Oh no, a

Boston cream." I paused, wondering if that was somehow dirty. I had probably crossed a line, but I didn't care. Because she was laughing and that was all that mattered.

Lake didn't laugh much these days.

"Okay, now I'm hungry and stressed."

"What's going on, Lake?" I asked, my voice serious this time.

"I have to travel for a retreat, and it's a big fucking deal, especially for a woman in my job, but thanks to the politics of it all, I have to bring a man with me. A date. Or I will be the old crone that showed up without a man. And if I do bring a man, then what is he, a boyfriend, a date, an escort? It's ridiculous, and I hate the fact that I'm even bothering about this. Because before everything happened, and no, I don't want to talk about it, but before, I would've just brought a friend or *him*. And it would've been fine. Well, not fine, but I wouldn't have even thought anything about it because he was a boyfriend. Or I would have a boyfriend, and it wouldn't be a big deal. But everyone else is either married or in serious relationships or bringing some escort or whatever. And I will have no one. Which I should be fine with, and I am fine with, but I can't be fine with."

She sounded out of breath when she finished speaking, and I could imagine her pacing around her living room and moving her hands while rambling. It was a very Lake thing to do.

"Okay, first, the more you say 'fine,' the more I believe that you're not anywhere near fine."

"Shut up."

"So what is this thing?"

She explained about the retreat, the huge deal, and I blinked. "I've heard of that. That's a big fucking deal, Lake. Congratulations."

"Thanks. I mean, once I get over the fact that I'm worried about bringing a date with me, I'll actually be excited about it. It is a big deal. I'm going to be able to help so many more people because of it."

And, of course, that's what she would think of. Not herself, not making more money. Even though she had gobs of it already. No, it was about helping others.

Because that was Lake fucking Montgomery.

"So what is it, you need to bring someone with you so that way nobody will wonder why you're alone?" I cursed. "You know what I mean. Hell, I'm not dating anyone. Most of our friends aren't. It's just that time of our lives. Other people just need to get over it."

"I know. And it's not that I want to date someone, far from it. I don't want a relationship. I'm enjoying my family and my career and just trying to tackle everything that I'm doing. And you already know I have too much on my plate."

"Of course you do. I've told you that countless times."

"I know you do. You love throwing that in my face. But it doesn't matter right now. Because if I go alone, then that will be a slight against me. And it shouldn't matter, but it will. And I don't know what I'm supposed to do. It's not like I can bring a cousin. Because that will just be weirder."

"Why don't I go with you?" I blurted.

The silence was deafening, and I realized I'd actually said the words and not just thought them. What the fuck? I didn't want to go to this damn thing. It was so far out of my wheelhouse. It would make no sense. What the hell was I thinking?

I didn't want to go with Lake, to pretend to be her boyfriend, or just to be someone to stand next to her. I wasn't going to fit in there. I would be this big, tattooed man next to tiny little Lake in her business suits. What the hell would I add to that situation?

"Are you serious?" she asked, her voice breathy.

"Don't laugh. I'm sorry. I just blurted it. Just trying to fix things like usual. Ignore me."

More silence.

"That would actually be amazing, Nick, because I wouldn't have to worry about the whole family thing because technically we're not family."

It was a whole lot more than technically, but I wasn't going to say that.

"And if I were to bring anyone else—that I would have to meet in the next week—that would be really weird because they don't know me, or they would put too much into the situation. Because there are guys I could ask at work, but then they would either think that I was hitting on them as their boss, or they would want something more. And it wouldn't be a problem with you. Because we're friends and we own a company together. This is perfect. It's like bringing a business partner with me. For a business thing. Oh, Nick, are you serious? I mean, I don't know about your appointments or anything, so maybe it won't work out, but if it would, it would mean the world. Seriously."

She kept going on, talking about the dates, the excitement lifting her voice and the stress slowly began to ease from her.

I couldn't back out now. Damn it. What the hell was wrong with me?

"I'll go. You need me, I'll be there. You know me, Lake. I always am."

"You are a lifesaver. Thank you so much, Nick. I'll email over the details, and we'll double check our schedules to make sure it'll really work. But oh my gosh, this is the best. Thank you."

We said a few more things and then she hung up,

and I knew she would literally be emailing me right now. She wouldn't wait, she would get her checklist, there would be a calendar, and then it would be done.

What the hell had I been thinking?

I set my phone down on the nightstand and rested my head in my hands.

Being alone with Lake was going to be a problem. And not just because we annoyed the fuck out of each other.

My doorbell rang and I frowned, with a strange notion thinking it could be Lake with a whole file folder of what I was expected to do. Not that she could work her magic that quickly, but you never knew. She was that amazing.

I stood up and slid a shirt over my head, since I wasn't about to answer the door shirtless just in case it *was* Lake.

Even though it wouldn't be.

I looked through the peephole and saw a woman with dark hair down around her shoulders, a worn face, with her hands folded in front of her.

For an instant, I didn't recognize her.

I opened the door, not sure why I was, but I couldn't leave her on the porch.

My mother had aged since I had last seen her, no sleep, too much stress, and the worry of who she had become.

She wasn't an alcoholic, wasn't a drug user. But she didn't take care of herself, and she sure as hell never took care of me.

"Nick. You answered the door. I want to…"

I just shook my head, then slammed the door.

Nope. Not going to do it. I wasn't even going to bother. She would get back in her car, and she would leave, and I would ignore her, just like she had ignored me.

I went back to the bedroom, checked my security readout to make sure she did indeed leave. Dejected, but I didn't care. I couldn't.

A message popped on my phone—a new email from Lake. I just shook my head.

Helping Lake like this would be a mistake.

Me being anywhere near Lake was always a fucking mistake.

Chapter 5

Lake

WHAT ON EARTH HAD I BEEN THINKING?

That question had rolled around my brain, knocking inside my skull, winding around my cerebellum, and slicing through my consciousness, since I had hung up the phone with Nick a few nights prior.

There had been no time for second chances or for backing away. Nick and I were both too stubborn to walk away now.

I had taken up Nick's blurted-out offer for him to travel with me.

Lake Montgomery and Nick Gatlin.

It didn't make any sense why he would even offer, other than pity.

Perhaps pity was the only reason that we got along these days.

But there was no going back, and I sat silently next to him in his vehicle on the way to Denver International Airport.

We would be on a nonstop flight to New York and then in a provided car to take us up to the Northern area. To upstate New York.

I often flew into bigger airports and then drove to my destination, and I had no idea if Nick would enjoy this or if he would groan the entire time.

Because as I sat next to him in silence, I was truly afraid that I didn't know Nick at all. And wasn't that a weird thing to be worried about?

"I checked in for us on the app, and I have our tickets with a QR code, so you don't have to worry."

He drummed his fingers on the steering wheel as he took the turn into long-term parking. "You've told me a couple of times. I have been on an airplane, you know. I might not be the world traveler that you are, but I do know that when we get on the plane, we only have to use the pedals when the pilot says to so we can really stay in the air."

My lips twitched. "I'll have you know that, hopefully, the plane should be a little more upgraded than that. We may have to turn with the plane when we bank or tilt backward or forwards during the landing and take-off, but I'm pretty sure they figured out the mechanics so we don't have to pedal. But you never know."

He snorted as he pulled into a space, and we got out of the car and grabbed our bags.

"You know any one of our friends or family would have dropped us off at the airport. You didn't have to leave your car here."

"I know, but they were all busy, and picking up and dropping off friends at the airport is one of the circles of hell, in my opinion, so I don't mind doing this."

"If you're sure."

I twisted my hands in front of myself, wondering why I was behaving like this. Why was I so nervous? It was just Nick.

"How many bags did you bring?" he grumbled as he pulled out both of my hard shells and his smaller bag.

I eyed the thing, frowning. "You have a suit in there?"

"Wait. I'm supposed to wear something other than jeans to this? I didn't sign up for that."

I knew he was joking, but I was a little nervous about everything, so I might have overreacted.

"Oh my God. It's okay. We can stop in the city and get you something."

"By the city, I assume you mean New York?"

"Of course I do. Oh hell, Nick. What are we doing?"

I hadn't actually meant to say that out loud.

"I am going to apparently go get some good food at this place that you mentioned, and I'm going to make sure men don't act like idiots, and I'm going to be there for my friend. I said I would do it, and here I am. Stop freaking out."

He slammed the back of his SUV, and somehow wielded all three bags. He also had a backpack slung over his shoulder, and took my carry-on, as well as my cross-body bag.

I might have overpacked, but honestly, there were so many different parts of this event that I had to dress for. It was part of my uniform, my mask. So I did what I had to, and frankly, I liked clothes and shoes. So people would just have to get over it.

"I'm sorry. And I'm grateful."

"If you say thank you one more time I'm going to have to hurt you. We're going to make a rule, you don't say thank you for this, and I don't complain about everything."

I raised a brow.

"Okay, fine, you're probably going to say thank

you, and I'm going to complain. It's just what we do. Come on, I know you want to be at the gate two hours early, so here we go."

"That is the recommended time."

"You would know," he grumbled.

Oh this was going to be great.

We stepped into the airport, everybody milling about, talking at once, the intercom and overhead voice saying something about baggage and terminal waits.

Nick's shoulders tensed immediately, but I kept moving, a pro at this.

When we noticed the line, Nick's jaw tensed, but I pulled him away from the back of the line.

"Come on, we're on this side."

"This is our airline."

"It is. But we're flying first-class, so we get a different line."

He looked down at the little red carpet then up at me.

"Are you serious right now?"

"I am serious. Now come on."

"I'm not riding first-class, Lake."

"Well I am. It's part of my business, and I want to. And my miles paid for this anyway. So come on."

"I cannot believe you," he grumbled, but I wasn't sure what exactly he was complaining about.

It was a shorter line over here, and as we checked in our bags and they went through our IDs, Nick was silent, and nodded when the ticket agent asked a few questions.

And then we were off through security, again in a different line, and we made our way to the gate area.

"Why did we have to be here two hours early if you were going to get the fancy experience?"

I gritted my teeth. "You never know. Sometimes I can't go through different parts of security, and DIA's security is always atrocious. Now, you can sit at the gates, or you can go get a beer or a drink in the lounge."

He looked at me, eyes wide. "Are you serious right now?" he asked, his voice low.

I held back a sigh. "Again, it comes with my credit card. I use it for work. I'm going to go into the lounge and sit down since there are no available seats at the gate. And you know that by the time that we get there, everybody is going to be grumbling anyway. We might as well just relax a bit."

He didn't say anything as I walked him into the lounge as my guest, and we sat down. I enjoyed myself a glass of champagne, and he grumbled, taking the beer that I offered him.

I didn't know what was wrong with him. This was what I did for work. I worked very hard for this. And I tried to treat my friends with what few amenities that I was able to.

But Nick didn't like it, and I didn't know why.

By the time an hour passed he hadn't spoken, but he had eaten thankfully. That seemed to relax him a bit, and then we were leaving the lounge, heading towards the gate.

We were in the first group, so we ended up in our seats together as we looked around and got comfortable.

"Thank you."

I looked at him, confused. "Why are you thanking me?"

"I hate flying. I hate feeling like a sardine and part of a herd of cattle. I realize that this probably cost you a pretty penny in terms of miles and whatever credit card fees you have, but I'm grateful. So thank you."

I relaxed as the flight attendant gave us a pre-flight beverage, and I sipped my champagne and stared over at Nick.

"I'm not always this fancy, you know. But we're going to a place where I have to be *The Lake Montgomery,* CEO. So I'm riding with it."

"Okay, so tell me exactly what I'm doing?"

We had talked a little bit about it, but I had also avoided some of it.

"We are headed to the Shiraz Shapley resorts. It's a

luxury five-star resort along the lines of the Ritz and the Four Seasons. It just isn't owned by that conglomerate."

"Okay," Nick growled a little lowly as we began to take off. He held onto the seat tightly, and that's when I realized it wasn't just that he hated flying, he was afraid of it, too. So I gripped his hand and he glared at me, but didn't push me away.

Something inside me did that little twisting thing, but I ignored it.

It was just nerves, after all.

"And what are we going to do there?"

"There are lunches and award ceremonies and golfing. There's games and meetings and presentations. It's pretty much just a place for the forty under forty to schmooze and to try to make connections and to preen like little peacocks." I grumbled as I said it, and he narrowed his eyes.

"You really don't want to be there, either."

I looked around the cabin to make sure that there wasn't anyone I recognized that was going to be there as well. Thankfully it all seemed to be different business people and families on their way to New York.

"No, I don't want to go. I find it weird that there's even an award for this because it's just age and how much you can accomplish with luck, hard work, and where you camc from."

"Your family name didn't help you with your brilliance in terms of that technology that you invented."

I froze, a little stunned that he would even say that.

"No, but I have a loving family who supported me in college, and were able to help me in after-school activities that led to this. So while we aren't old money, without my parents and their support, I wouldn't be here. And that's something I know is a privilege."

Nick nodded tightly. "You Montgomerys take care of each other. And anyone attached."

I held back a smile, because he wasn't talking about me just then.

"You're right. Those are the connections and networking we do. Within the family. So while we go here, I'm going to meet people who I'm not going to like, and hopefully some people that I do. There are two men that I know I'm not going to get along with already because I've had to go to conventions with them."

Nick narrowed his gaze at me, but before I could say anything, the flight attendant came and we gave our lunch and drink orders.

Nick shook his head, his lips twitching as the flight attendant continued behind us.

"This is ridiculous."

"Not really. Everybody should be fed and have drinks while they're on a plane. It's the company's

CEOs and their money pinching that're the problem. No matter what seat you are in, you shouldn't go hungry or thirsty or feel like you're going to have a seizure because you're stuck with your back so straight. I have the privilege to get something like this, and even then, it's not like it used to be."

"Well, that puts me in my place."

"Shut up," I grumbled.

"Okay, who are these guys?"

This time his voice went stony.

"There's a man named Joseph and another man named Ned. They're both in the same field I am, and they don't like the fact that I do well for myself. They've put it plain, and usually try to make me feel like the little woman."

"And I'm not allowed to hurt them?"

I froze. "Don't punch them, don't growl at them. Not that you ever actually use violence like that."

"I've hit a man or two in my life."

"In a bar fight?" I teased.

"Maybe. You don't know me that well, Lake."

I narrowed my gaze. "We own a business together, and you're my cousin's best friend. I'm pretty sure I know you well, Nick."

"Whatever you say, Lake."

Our gazes clashed for an instant before the flight

attendant handed us our drinks. I chugged my water, grateful I had asked for that as well as a cocktail.

"Is there anybody here you're going to like? Or is this going to be a pain for you, too?"

I hadn't missed the fact that he included this being a pain for him. Oh this was going to be a lovely trip.

"There's a woman named Susanna." My voice brightened as I said it, and Nick tilted his head, studying me. "She's an amazing woman who has paved the way for people like me and others. She turns forty this year, therefore I'll only see her at other events. Not one where ageism comes into play."

"What makes her so special?"

"She's a woman in business who kicks ass. She has four kids and a loving husband. And everybody there like Joseph and Ned talk shit about her behind her back because they're afraid of her. I just want to be her."

He stared at me then, confusion etched on his face. "Why are you doing this? Why are you even taking this trip? Why do you even need me to come when I know you can handle anything?"

I pressed my lips together, his words comforting even as they worried me for some reason. "I need to show my face and show the world. And I need to provide more for these companies that I work with. Like

Diana and her fun vampire café." I explained it to him earlier and he was already on board. "It's going to make great money and do well, but she needs startup capital after losing her husband so I'm going to do what I can. I'm going to help others, and if I need to save face and put on a fake smile to gain what accolades I can so I can network my way into helping others? I'll do it."

He nodded, stared at me, and sighed.

"Okay then. I'll be the guy there so they don't ask questions, they don't have any ammunition against you. I got it."

I smiled, relieved that he really did get it, and as we were served our lunch, and we spoke about the tattoo shop and other things that weren't important, I wondered exactly how this weekend would go. Because things would change. They had to. I just didn't know how yet.

Getting our bags from the airport took forever since baggage claim was always a pain in the ass. Our driver stuffed everything into a large black SUV, and then Nick and I were in the back seat, not speaking as we went through our phones. I had a thousand emails to go through, and Nick did too. He owned a business after all, and he was dealing with clients who would want to work with him as soon as he got back. While on the plane he'd pulled out his notepad and drawn a few things, his mind going a mile a minute.

I had always been envious of his talents, and though I didn't have any of his ink on my skin, I figured one day I would. I would have ink from every one of the artists that worked at Montgomery Ink Legacy. It was my legacy too, even if I hadn't always meant it to be.

We pulled in front of the Shiraz Shapley hotel and resort, and Nick whistled low under his breath as we got out.

I looked up at the gorgeous hotel that was out of a dream, with the green grounds and luxurious trees, and shook my head.

"I've never been here before, but I've heard about it. There's real Italian marble here."

"I'm dressed in my best shoes right now, and new jeans, and I feel like I'm going to get this place dirty."

I looked at those jeans that hugged his ass and thighs, and his gray-blue Henley that showcased his eyes, and I swallowed hard.

I hadn't really noticed what he was wearing before because I was nervous, but now I really needed to pull my gaze away from his body. There was something wrong with me.

"You look fine. It's travel day. We all look casual."

He looked down at my white jumpsuit, my strappy sandals, and my fully done hair and makeup.

"That's you casual?"

"It's a jumpsuit. I'm not wearing slacks and a top and a sports jacket."

"I brought a sports jacket."

I looked down at his small bag that was now being wheeled away to the lobby and front desk.

"In that?"

Nick laughed. "Yes, in that. Don't worry. It won't be wrinkled."

"Just making sure."

We made our way into the lobby to check-in, when the one person I honestly didn't want to see stepped in front of me.

"Lake, it's so good to see you," Joseph sneered.

I stood straight as Nick took in the situation and held out his elbow. I knew he had done it on purpose, and I didn't even realize I was moving my hand until I placed my fingers along the inside of his arm, keeping myself steady.

Joseph noticed and raised a brow.

"Hello, Joseph. They said you would be here."

"Asking about me, were you?"

"Only so I knew if I needed to bring disinfectant."

Nick smiled at my side while Joseph glared.

"Well, they always need to add the riff-raff here. It wouldn't be the feminist movement without letting in a couple of women. Now we get to see what happens next."

He left while Nick held back a growl, and I counted to ten inside my head, a panic attack kept trying to rear its ugly head.

I didn't realize Nick had moved until his finger was underneath my chin trying to lift my head up.

I ignored the heat of him, breathing hard.

"You with me?"

I nodded, my pulse racing.

"I hate him. I shouldn't have thrown that last bit at him."

"It was hot."

I blinked, wondering why he had said that, but then I realized that my pulse was racing for an entirely different reason, and he must have done that on purpose. Just to screw with me, and to pull me out of my funk.

"Let's go check into our rooms. I'm tired."

"And I'm sure you need to—what is it called—freshen up for dinner?"

"Pretty much," I said with a laugh, and we made our way to check-in.

This place was highly efficient and didn't keep people waiting. The woman behind the desk smiled at me.

"Hello, Lake Montgomery. Two rooms."

"Of course, Ms. Montgomery. Let me check."

There was that familiar tapping of keys, even

though they always seemed so loud at any hotel, no matter the cost of the rooms.

Lots of clicking and clacking, as the woman frowned slightly, barely visible, before she smiled up at me.

"I'm sorry, this was underneath the room block for the event, correct?"

I nodded, as the only way you could book this week was through the event.

"Yes. Lake Montgomery."

"Would the other room be under your guest's name?"

Nick frowned. "Nick Gatlin."

"Let me check."

Again, with the clicking and clacking, as another guest in a suit got in line behind me, one I recognized as a man who owned a Fortune 500 company.

I nodded at him and turned back to focus on what was going on in front of me.

"I'm so sorry. It seems we only have one reservation. It could be that the event canceled the second one; this is a large event, and they only have one room per group. I'm sorry."

I blinked and looked up at Nick but was aware if I didn't move on quickly, people would stare and say things, and I didn't have time for that.

"That's fine." I looked up at Nick. "Right?"

"Of course. We can make it work."

I heard the growl in his voice, though, and knew that it wasn't fine.

Damn it.

"We have your corner suite with a king."

"Oh, do you have two queens?" I asked, my voice a squeak.

Nick stiffened beside me as the woman continued to type.

"I'm sorry. Just a king. Will that be okay?"

Another high-powered CEO got into line after the other man, and I nodded tightly, knowing there was no way out of this. I was not about to make a scene.

I smiled at the woman. "Of course. One room. One bed. Perfect." I muttered that last part as Nick let out a pained wheeze, and I signed my name on the tablet in front of me.

She handed us our keys, and I turned, smiling at the other people in the lobby, before making my way to the elevator.

"Are you serious right now?" Nick growled.

"I'm sure there's a couch. I'll take the couch."

"You're not taking the fucking couch," he growled.

I pressed my key to the inside of the elevator to get to our floor, my hands shaking. "I'm sorry. This isn't exactly what I was planning."

"If I thought you were planning this entire

annoying trip just to get me into bed, I would say something. There are easier ways to get me into bed, Lake."

I nearly tripped over my own heels as we made our way onto the floor.

"Nick," I snapped.

"It's fine. I'm sure there's a sofa bed."

"Not at this hotel," I grumbled, and I opened the door into the suite, knowing our bags would show up later. I stared at the immaculate and ostentatious room, at the small couch in the corner that could not hold a bed inside, and the grandiose king-size bed past the double doors on the other side of the living area.

I stared at Nick, then at the bed, and knew that all of my past mistakes had come back to bite me in the ass.

And this weekend had just gotten a little longer.

Chapter 6

Nick

THE SOUND OF LAKE GETTING READY IN THE BATHROOM was the only thing I could focus on. Considering the beat of my heart echoing in my ears was deafening, the fact that I could hear her at all said something.

There hadn't been a pullout couch, just two loveseats and a semi-couch that wasn't long enough for me. I had nearly had to physically toss Lake into the bed so that way she wouldn't touch the couch. Then I remembered that I didn't touch her, and she would have issues if any man did.

My hands fisted on my stomach and I let out a

breath, telling myself that growling would only freak her out. And while I couldn't find Zach and beat him up, I could at least pretend.

I slept on the damn couch that was comfortable—honestly more comfortable than my bed at home—but was too small.

After we had gotten into the room and gotten settled, we had dinner with a few people who I couldn't remember more than their names. I was decent with names because I had to be in my job. Forgetting somebody's name as I was literally driving a needle into their skin repeatedly seemed like an asshole thing to do.

So I schmoozed the best way I could, meaning I stayed silent after she introduced me and answered questions from a couple of men that Lake seemed relaxed around, though it was still a different Lake than I was used to.

There were different versions of the Lake that had been in my mind since I had met her.

The one who had hidden behind her hair when she had been a child and was still getting used to her new family, just like I was getting used to mine, but in completely different contexts.

The shy one who loved books and science and coding.

There was the woman who laughed and drank and

joked around with us in our friend group. The woman who owned part of the shop and came in to joke around, even in high heels and pencil skirts that made her ass look delectable, was still relaxed.

Then there was this business Lake, but then again, this seemed like a different version of the woman that I had seen at her company headquarters the one time I visited with Leif. We had gone to drop some paperwork off, and I had seen her in her element, a CEO, helping others but also dominating the workforce in a kind yet forceful way.

She was brilliant, not egotistical, but confident. Hell, I had more of an ego in my job than she did, but the person I had seen yesterday at dinner had been a shade of that. The polite CEO was testing the waters of the people around her. And I had been quiet, trying to be nice and watching her.

Today was the pre-award ceremony, a lunch event that was probably going to give me a migraine.

But I was here, being her friend, because there was nothing else I knew how to do.

When that asshole had spoken to her the day before, she had tried her best to stand up to him. Oh, she had done it. She had cut him down to size in a way that I knew the man would try to retaliate later. But I had also seen her on the verge of a panic attack. Something I had seen before. She was good at hiding it, and I wasn't even sure her family knew about it.

But I had made an accidental habit of watching Lake Montgomery.

And that meant I noticed when her face had paled slightly beneath her reddened cheeks, the way that she had pressed her lips together, and I could see her finger pressing against her thumb, counting out to ten.

All so she could catch her breath and not panic in public.

I knew she had gone to therapy in the past, even before the events with Zach. So I didn't know where exactly those attacks had come from, but damn it, something was wrong, and I knew it wasn't my place to deal with it. But I wanted to.

I wanted to fix it.

But it wasn't like it was my job to fix it.

I sat up as my phone buzzed, and I took it from the table, snorting at the text chain from the guys.

Leif: *Are you awake yet? How's the resort?*

Sebastian: *Take photos. I need to live vicariously through you because I can never afford that. Do you know how much college costs? And I'm not talking about my own.*

Noah: *How's Lake doing? Send photos. The sisters want to see it.*

I shook my head and answered back, wondering why they were texting so damn early in the morning their time, but I was running late. I slept in because we had been out late, and now I didn't want to get up and shower because Lake was in there. And there were just some things I didn't need to be part of.

Me: *I'm afraid to break anything. There's marble and crystal everywhere. I'm pretty sure there are more diamonds in this place on random necks than I've ever seen in my life. But Lake is kicking ass.*

Leif: *I'm glad you're there for her. I don't understand that whole lifestyle, but Brooke has to deal with some of it in her job. So I can only imagine the dude-bros that she has to deal with.*

Me: *I almost punched a guy yesterday, but your cousin took care of it.*

The fact that I was saying your cousin rather than Lake meant I was putting distance there for a reason. A reason I did not need to go into.

Sebastian: *What happened? Is Lake okay?*

Noah: *I can get on a plane. I mean, I think I can. But I will.*

I held back a curse, annoyed with myself for even saying that. I had just been damn proud of the way Lake had handled it, and I didn't need to worry them. Lake could handle this on her own. I was just there as support. A marble pillar that didn't need to speak.

And why did that sound grumbly?

Me: *Everything's fine. Just normal. Guys trying to think that they're big and bad for the little woman. You know Lake*

*doesn't put up with that. None of the girls do. And should I be
calling them girls if I'm talking about things like this?*

My lips twitched as the guys continued to text
back, going on about whether we should call them the
girls even though they also called themselves "the
girls."

We were just fucking around because we respect
our friends, our family. I was here for a reason, after
all. Because I did respect Lake. And I knew she could
do anything she put her mind to.

Leif: *Brooke and I want to know what the schedule is for
the day.*

I smiled.

Me: *I like how you guys are a 'we'. It's cute.*

Leif: **Middle finger emoji.**

Leif: *Shut up.*

Me: *I think today is lunch and maybe a meeting or two.
We're not doing the golf thing this morning.*

Sebastian: *Should I be worried that you just said 'we'?*

I winced, holding back another curse so Lake
didn't hear me and come out and wonder what the hell
we were talking about.

Me: *Shut up. With Lake, damn it. You know that.*

Noah: *Whatever. I know you will take care of our cousin.
You're one of us after all.*

I said my goodbyes as they all headed into their
own lives, and I sighed.

I was one of them. Lake was practically family. I didn't know why I was acting like this.

Oh, I did. I knew exactly why I was feeling like this, thinking like this. I had for years, even though I had told myself I didn't.

First off, she was younger, and she was Leif's cousin, practically his sister. And since Leif called me practically his brother, that would have been weird. And there was no way I would ever fit into the sphere of Lake.

We were in such different worlds that I felt out of place, even sleeping on a couch. Like I wasn't even clean enough for it.

I just needed to get this done, go home, and never think about it again.

The double doors to the bathroom opened and she walked out, her hair done perfectly, her makeup expertly done, and she smiled at me.

She had on white linen pants and this flowy top that emphasized her waist but covered her breasts. Conservative as possible but still womanly.

She had bare feet, and she had painted her toenails white, making her feet look tanned. Why was I staring at her feet?

And why did I care about her curves?

"Oh good, you're up. I ordered breakfast, and it should be here soon. I know what you like. But if you want to change your mind, let me know. I just didn't want to bother you."

I cleared my throat, set the phone down on the table, and got up, stretching my back.

"That's fine. I'll eat whatever. I should go shower."

"Of course." Lake pulled her gaze to my eyes, and I wondered what she was looking at. Or maybe I was just tired and seeing things.

"We can take turns. I'll sleep on the couch. And damn it, the bed is huge. We can put a pillow barrier between us and sleep next to each other. It won't be too bad."

Thankfully my pants were baggy enough that she didn't notice the fact that my cock had hardened at that thought. I already had morning wood, and I was getting harder thinking about sleeping next to Lake.

No, that wouldn't be fucking happening.

"It's fine. It's comfier than my bed at home."

She gave me a dubious look. "That means we need to get you a different bed."

"Don't you fucking buy me a bed. I can handle things on my own."

She frowned and held out both hands. "I meant I would pick it out for you and be a dork while you paid for it. You and I have never had an issue with money before. Please don't make one now. We co-own a business. Equal parts."

"There's always going to be a thing about money, Lake. We're in completely different circles. You know that."

"Oh, shut up. You never had an issue before. Now one night sleeping on a couch in this suite and we have a problem? No, you're sleeping in the bed."

"No, I'm not. I'm not sleeping with you or in the bed."

I froze as I said the words before I winced. "I'm sorry. I need coffee."

"Yes, you do. And frankly, so do I." She looked down at her watch. We have the lunch ceremony with the keynote later, but they're still milling about and networking. I know you already set out your clothes, and they actually match mine nicely. You know, I almost asked you if we should coordinate our outfits, then I realized that would just be weird, even if we were together."

Why the hell did she keep bringing that up?

"It's fine. I'll be quick. I don't have as much hair as you."

"I did notice you got a haircut before this."

I ran my hand through my hair and shrugged. "Needed a trim. Figured I shouldn't look like a mountain man."

"You can look however you want. I'm the one that has to care about my own things. And that's on me."

I snorted as I made my way into the bedroom and the bathroom. "I see the way these vultures are. You're not like them. But you do need to at least be a chameleon. I won't shame you."

She reached out and gripped my arm as I passed her. I froze and looked down to where her hand touched my skin.

"You would never shame me, Nick. I'm sorry if this whole thing's uncomfortable for you. I'm not exactly in my element here. I know I may look it sometimes, but I'm not. So thank you. For doing this."

I nodded tightly, then went to the shower, knowing that not even a cold shower was going to help.

THE LUNCH WENT DECENTLY, AS WE SAT WITH THREE other couples who were pleasant enough but all knew each other very well, and while they tried to include Lake in the conversation, it was a little stilted.

But the food was damn good, so at least there was that.

Lake had even commented as much under her breath, and I smiled, liking the way that it lit up her eyes when she joked.

When we finished lunch, everyone walked out onto the veranda for an afternoon cocktail hour. People

were schmoozing, talking, and congratulating themselves on this accomplishment.

I knew Lake was amazing. She was brilliant and
deserved everything that came to her. Yet this just felt
weird as hell.

Mostly because everybody came from different
industries, so I didn't know where we all fit in.

Joseph, that growly asshole guy from before, came
over to us, another man next to him who leered at
Lake.

She stiffened at my side for an instant before she
lifted her chin and smiled.

"Lake, so good that you're here." The guy grinned
down at her, trying to check out her cleavage, and I
stepped forward slightly, since I was bigger than both
of them.

The man glared at me, and Lake cleared her
throat.

"Ned, this is my friend, Nick. I don't believe you
two have been introduced."

Ned, the dumbass that she had warned me about.
Well, he was lucky I didn't punch him right then just
because I felt like it.

"Friend? Really?" Ned asked. "I'm surprised you
didn't bring Zach with you."

Wrong thing to say. My chest tightened, and I tried
to move forward, but Lake was there, pressing her

hand against my back as she leaned into me. If anyone didn't know her well, they would think she was fine, that she was confident and could take anything.

But I saw the tension in her shoulders and her jaw, so I slid my arm around her, so we were hugging each other as she stared up at the man.

"I've no idea where Zach is, but I'm sure he's enjoying himself. That's what he does. I see your wives are over there, alone. You should probably go with them."

With that, she turned and left. I followed after glaring at the two men.

They shrugged before watching her walk away, and all I wanted to do was punch them. But that wouldn't help anything.

They were just good at snide remarks and bringing up Zach like they had any right to.

A woman with a low-cut dress, big red hair, and redder lips smiled at me as I walked past.

"You're new," she purred before Lake pulled at my arm.

I looked down at Lake, and she mouthed "Ned's wife," and I rolled my eyes before I took Lake's hand, and we moved away.

"Was she serious?" I mumbled.

"She and Ned have a bet at these things to see how many people each of them can sleep with. And then they go home and fight about it and probably fuck like bunnies." She shuddered as she said it and I nearly gagged.

"I really need something to drink right now. Like bourbon."

"Did somebody say bourbon?" A woman with dark hair and light eyes said as she came forward.

Lake's entire body relaxed, and she smiled wide, one of the first genuine smiles I'd seen all weekend.

"Susanna."

"Lake. It's so good to see you."

Susanna. This was the other woman nominated and awarded this weekend. The woman that Lake admired and looked up to.

She seemed genuine, and as the two hugged, I finally got it. Why she came to this damn thing.

Because she deserved this, and not everybody were assholes. Although the ratio wasn't great.

"I'm so glad that you're here," Lake whispered, even though I could hear it.

"I'm so glad that I'm here too. Now introduce me to your gentleman here."

Lake laughed and gestured toward me.

"This is Nick. My friend. He owns part of Montgomery Ink Legacy with me."

Susanna's eyes brightened as she looked me up and

down. Not in a creepy way, but in a way that said that she was watching out for her friend.

I lifted my chin in acknowledgment and smiled, and our gazes met. She smiled widely back, and I figured I had just found an ally.

Interesting.

"Okay, I'm just so happy to see you. Really."

"Jamie's coming, and I know he went to go find bourbon. They only have this rum drink here because one of the guys owns a distillery, but we'll find the good stuff."

"I don't mind rum, but if it's Bradley's Rum, I'm going to go with no," Lake joked as she sneered the word Bradley.

The two women's gazes met before they laughed, and a man with a wide chest, all muscle, and dark hair with gray at the temples came forward.

"They gave me a bottle, and since I saw you over here with your best friend and her date, I brought four glasses."

He set them down on the side table between us and held out his hand.

"Hello, I'm Jamie McAvoy. It's nice to meet you."

Jamie McAvoy. I knew him. A former defensive end for an NFL team. And that meant I knew of his wife as well, her company, and the charities that she did around the world.

I had even given to her charity before. "Susanna McAvoy. I know you."

She winked. "I guess I need to know you as well. Now, let's have a toast, some really good bourbon, and I have an idea for a school that I wanted to talk to you about."

I frowned as Lake beamed.

She leaned forward, brightening to the point it did something to me I didn't want to think about. "Oh, the one that we were emailing about? Do you have more information?"

"Oh yes. I want to discuss building that school completely, plus we have to go through our programs that are going to help the Live Foundation."

I frowned, going through what I remembered about the Live Foundation.

It was a foundation that helped women thrive in business, life, and health. Lake was not a founder but a heavy supporter.

They spoke, and I drank damn fine bourbon and listened to one of my favorite NFL players talk, and it sounded like the two women were going to take over the world.

She was fucking amazing.

Brilliant, caring, and had her hands in a thousand different pies, protecting the world even as she gave herself to it.

And who the hell was I?

Then again, did it matter?

I was in trouble, and I knew it. I couldn't sit here for much longer, not if I needed to be normal for dinner and the awards ceremony.

I cleared my throat after Jamie was called away on another thing, and I stood up.

"I've got to go," I growled out, and for once I saw a hurt look cross over Lake's face, before she blinked it away, and she nodded.

"Of course. I'll be back soon."

"No, it's fine. Take your time. This is your thing. Do it. I've just got to go."

And I walked away, leaving her behind.

The one thing I knew I'd gotten right.

Chapter 7

Lake

I SLID MY HANDS DOWN THE EVENING DRESS, THE SILK and lace a contradiction against my skin.

Finding the right balance between looking professional, elegant, feminine, yet powerful wasn't easy all the time. I constantly searched what others wore and what made me feel good.

It wasn't that I cared what others thought, but I needed to. Because I had people who depended on me. And if I looked like I was trying too hard or not trying hard enough, it could affect others' livelihoods.

A simple dress where I looked like I was trying to

walk across the Venice Festival to showcase a movie meant that others would talk. If I wore a pantsuit, others would talk. If I wore a dress that didn't make me feel like I was powerful, I would talk.

I liked feeling pretty. And there was nothing wrong with that.

I was keeping with my creams and whites as my color palette for the event. I hadn't meant to dress in all the same colors, but it was my mood. I liked the look, and I was nervous.

I would go up and give a small speech to thank those who nominated me to be here. And then I would sit down and watch others do the same.

And while I appreciated the event and the excuse to dress up in a way that I didn't normally get to, I had already achieved what I had wanted to by coming here.

I met with Susanna and eight other CEOs who all had pledged to help with some of the charities I worked with.

These were the networking opportunities that I had come for. That and the larger scale ones that Susanna and I would be working on.

We had a lot to accomplish, but had done so much already in these past couple of days.

And I knew with the connections that I had formed through lunches and drinks and casual conversations in a hotel lobby that I had made something of myself from just this one event. Yes, it was networking at its finest, and it was rude sometimes, and ridiculous, but I was going to help people.

I was allowed to kick ass in business. I was allowed to love my job and do well at it. Even if some of the world thought that women shouldn't.

I frowned and fixed my lipstick.

And that was enough of that. I didn't need to get on my high horse, not when I had other things to worry about.

Namely, Nick.

Something was wrong with him. He had growled and had walked away, and we hadn't spoken since. Yes, I had things to do, and he had gone to work on his art, but something was wrong.

And yet, this was my night. I was grateful that he was here. I was grateful that nobody really questioned his presence. They just assumed I was dating him. Nobody cared that we weren't married, not that we ever would be. Nobody cared, because he was my buffer.

Tonight was about me. And I was allowed to have it be about me.

I didn't have time to placate him and worry only about him. I had done that for someone else, and I wouldn't do it again.

Zach had always made me feel like crap and pushed me down and I hadn't even realized he was doing it for a long time.

Because his needs were first, and if I wasn't doing what he wanted, then he would yell at me, or treat me like crap, or persuade me to do what he wanted.

And for a moment, I thought Nick was doing the same, and while he hadn't been, it had been too close for comfort.

I sighed, grabbed my purse, and knew I needed to talk to him. But not tonight. Tonight was about something else.

Tonight was about an award that I would be happy to get, even if it came with strings.

I walked out of the bathroom, through the bedroom to the living room, where he had gotten dressed.

I froze, looking at him in his tux, and blinked. "How did you fit that in your suitcase?"

He looked up at me then, his hands going down his lapels. He was all broad and muscled and beautiful.

There was something really wrong with me. I couldn't help it. I had always been attracted to Nick. Which had been a problem, but we were friends, so it wasn't a big deal. I was allowed to think he was hot, but damn it, why did he have to look so good in a tux?

The thing looked as if it had been molded to him, and I could barely breathe.

He cleared his throat. "I didn't own one, but I actually talked to your dad about it, mostly because if anyone in your family or our group of friends knew how to get a tux, it would be him."

I held back a smile. My dad was a former model and now was a bestselling author and Oscar winner for screenplays. We didn't talk about it much because I wasn't an LA kid or anything like that, but yes, my dad knew all about tuxes.

"Wait, when did you talk to my dad about this? And what does that have to do with you having a tux right now?"

"I didn't have much time to get one custom-made. So I am wearing one from a shop he took me to, and I bought it, don't worry. But it needed alterations because, apparently, my shoulders are like a line-backer's."

I barely resisted the urge to lick my lips. Because yes, his shoulders were broad. But that was beside the point.

I was still so confused, so I blamed that for my wayward thoughts on Nick in a freaking tux. "Wait, did my dad ship this to you?"

Nick fidgeted, shoved his hands in his pockets, and

then pulled them back out as if he didn't want to leave creases.

"Yes. And he said I could ship it back to him if I can't fit it in my bag. It was the only suitcase I had. I told you, I don't travel much, and if I do, it's usually a duffle. But yeah, I got a tux. Didn't want to shame you."

I moved forward, frowning at the odd tone in his voice. "You wouldn't shame me. Honestly. You could have shown up in jeans to this for all I care. Which I know sounds the exact opposite of what I would normally say, but I'm glad you're here." I knew I still needed to talk to him about what happened before. I couldn't hide in my own feelings all the time.

"Before we go down there, I wanted to tell you something."

I froze, memories of Zach hitting me again.

"I'm sorry."

I blinked, confused. "What?"

"I'm sorry. I'm not good at this, and I nearly ruined it. I was in my head and left when I shouldn't have. I shouldn't have taken out my own feelings on you. Even though they're just dumbass feelings. I promise I won't be an asshole tonight. I can't promise I won't ever be one again. That would be a lie." His lips twitched and I smiled. "But I am sorry for leaving you hanging because of my own needs. You didn't deserve that."

I was floored. Seriously floored.

Zach had never done anything like that. He never apologized, had never even gone into the realm of being sorry.

I just…I couldn't focus. And why was I comparing those two?

Zach had nothing on Nick, and Nick wasn't my boyfriend or anything. Why was my brain doing that?

Nick frowned before he took a step and blinked, his gaze going down my body, his eyes so heated that I nearly blushed, wanting to press my thighs together.

"Fuck. I didn't say that before because, like I said, I was in my head, but damn it. You look amazing. I guess you clean up nicely, Montgomery." He cleared his throat and put his hands back in his pockets.

Why did it feel like when he said Montgomery, it was to remind him of who I was?

And where had that come from? Damn it. I could not think like that.

This was just a night that we were dressed up like we were going to prom. As friends. Practically cousins.

Not kissing ones.

Don't think about kissing.

I laughed awkwardly. "Oh, well, thank you. And, you look great too. I mean, I've never seen you in a tux."

"I've seen you in dresses, Lake. This one's different. You look fancy."

I froze, putting my hands on my hips. "Too fancy? I brought an extra dress, just in case I was going overboard, but everyone else is in tuxes, and all the wives are in ball gowns. I thought about wearing a tux too, but then I realized I liked dresses more so…"

"You look fine, Lake."

"You said it was better than fine before," I grumbled.

"I'm not going to win this conversation, so are you ready to go?"

I took a step forward, then put my hand over my chest, my fingers brushing my neck.

His gaze went to that motion, and I remembered the last times my fingers were touching my neck in front of him. When I had gone to him for help.

No, I wasn't going to think about that. Because that didn't matter. Zach didn't matter in this moment.

"I need help with this stupid necklace. Can you help me? I know your hands are big, but you work with a tiny needle all day. You should be fine."

I winced as I said it, rambling, and he narrowed his gaze, his pupils dilating.

Was it suddenly hot in here? Was I losing my mind?

He let out a deep growl, his chest rumbling, or maybe I was just imagining things. It wasn't like he was a werewolf in some shifter romance. He was just Nick. Tattoo artist, friend, practically my cousin.

And if I kept calling him my cousin, it was going to get weird really fucking quick.

I turned when he held up a finger and spun it in a circle, and then he slid the necklace over my neck, his calloused fingertips brushing along my skin. I pressed my lips together, trying to breathe through my nose, trying not to hyperventilate.

But he worked the clasp quickly, and I swallowed hard, the heat between us pulsating.

It was just my imagination.

It had to be.

"You ready?" he asked after a moment before he cleared his throat.

I nodded and turned, both of us staring at one another, his deep breaths in sync with mine.

"I'm ready."

He held out his elbow, and I took it with my fingers, grabbing my purse with my free hand, and I followed him.

I was going to walk downstairs in a gorgeous dress, feeling like a princess, and my panties were damp.

I was in such fucking trouble.

THE AWARD CEREMONY WENT QUICKLY, AND I BARELY remembered what I said. Thankfully I had had a speech written, so I just needed to recite it word for word, smile, take a photo, and then sit back down and eat.

We sat with Susanna and her husband, so Nick had someone to talk to. I liked football, but I didn't like it as much as Nick apparently did. So he was happy, and I was trying to scramble to find two brain cells to work together.

When the dancing began and people went out to the dance floor to do random versions of the chicken dance and other things that nobody ever needed to see me do, I stood up and grabbed my purse.

"I need to powder my nose. I'll be right back."

Nick snorted into his beer and I rolled my eyes.

"Fine. I need to use the restroom. Better?"

"It's just me, Montgomery. You can say what you want."

I rolled my eyes and caught the glance between Susanna and her husband, but I ignored it. I passed by a few other couples, smiled at them, and made my way to the restroom area.

I nearly tripped over my feet as Ned and Joseph stood there, both of them vaping. They blew smoke in my face, and I coughed at the marijuana smell. I didn't care what they did, but I didn't want to be part of it.

"Excuse me."

"No, how about you excuse me." Ned came closer and I backed up. I shouldn't have done that, but it was instinct. I pressed my back to the wall, as he hovered over me and grinned.

"You always think you're too good for us. All high and mighty in your little silver tower. But nobody cares about fucking Colorado. You're nothing. You're not in the big cities. You just pretend that you know what you're doing in the Mile High City. You always think you're better than me. Won't even give me the time of day. But I see the way you watch me. I see the way that you lick your lips when I'm around. You want me."

I smelled the booze on his breath, the whiskey tainting his lips along with whatever he had just smoked.

Joseph giggled behind him, too far gone to care.

And then Ned was closer, his hand brushing my shoulder, and I put my own hand on his chest.

"Don't."

"Don't what?"

He leaned forward, his hand going lower, and I pressed again.

But then Ned was on the floor, holding his bleeding lip, and Nick was standing there.

I blinked as Nick stalked forward, ready to punch the man again. I pulled him back, holding his elbow.

"Stop."

Nick looked at me. "What?"

"Don't."

Mortification set in as others came forward, and Ned's wife came to his side. "I'm sorry. I'll watch him better. Damn it. I knew he was going to get another bloody lip. Every time." She dragged him back, Joseph going with them.

I just stood there as people started whispering. And I stared at Nick, at the way that he shook out his hand.

"I don't know."

I wasn't even sure what I was saying, but then others were staring at me. Not at Nick.

Because Nick hadn't done anything wrong. Had he?

No, I was the one who hadn't been able to take care of myself. I was the one who people were staring at. And as the panic set in, I turned on my heel and left, knowing I couldn't let anybody see this. I couldn't let them see me break.

I couldn't let Nick see me break.

Chapter 8

Nick

I FUCKED UP. NOT JUST A LITTLE BIT. A FULL-BLOWN fuck-up that I wasn't going to be able to fix.

But damn it, what the hell was I supposed to do?

I followed Lake through the corridor and took a separate elevator since she had already made it up.

I didn't know how I was going to make this better. If I could make this better. I had already spent that day trying to atone for me being an asshole while thinking about how much better she was than me. And it had all gone to hell.

All because I couldn't think. Someone had touched her. Had threatened to hurt her.

Of course, I was going to do something about it.

I stepped off the elevator and made my way to the door, opening it with a harsh click, knowing that if I didn't calm down I would just make things worse.

"Are you serious right now?" Lake asked as she whirled on me.

I stiffened, the door closing behind me.

"I'm sorry for making a scene. But he touched you."

I hadn't meant to practically shout the words, but there was no going back from them.

"You didn't need to hit him!"

She tossed her purse on the couch, the same place that I was sleeping this weekend because I didn't have my own fucking bed.

"Yes the fuck I did. I'm not some candy-ass. I know words work well in some cases, and I fucking use them if I have to. But that man didn't care. And you know if you reported him, nothing would happen. From the way that he acts, nothing has ever happened. *You know it.*"

I hadn't meant to emphasize the last words, and when she paled, the heat pulled out of me. I moved forward, hands outstretched.

"Fuck. I'm sorry, Lake."

We both knew what I was sorry for this time. For Zach. Not for that asshole in the corridor that we wouldn't think about again.

"No, no," she said, hands outstretched this time, though neither one of us was touching the other.

"Lake."

"I'm sorry for bringing you here and acting as if I belong here, too. Because I don't. I'm the kid who didn't feel like a Montgomery forever, and then when I finally did, I went and did a different job than anyone else and feel left out. I'm going to come here and be the odd woman out. Because it's what I do. I'm an idiot and didn't think about the fact that Ned was prowling the corridors. And I didn't push back. I didn't fight for myself. That's what's wrong here. Not you hitting him. Because, damn, it's fine. It's what I should have done. And that's what I'm pissed off at."

I was floored and tried to get through exactly what she just said because there was so much wrong with it I could barely focus.

"What the hell? What the hell is wrong with you?"

She opened her mouth to speak, and I realized I probably could have said that better.

"No. You have always been the center. The center of the Montgomerys, everything. You are the center. At least the center of me."

She looked at me, slack-jawed, and I backpedaled. "Fuck. I didn't mean that."

"What are you talking about?"

"It's fine. You belong here. You belong with the family, you belong everywhere. I don't know why you're having such self-doubt, and if it's because of that asshole, then I want to find him and beat the hell out of him. But damn it, Lake. You make it hard to think. You've always made it hard to think. And that's the damn problem."

I didn't realize we were standing so close until I could feel the heat of her, and my head was bent just slightly. And when she looked up at me, mouth parted, I did the stupidest thing possible.

I leaned down, crushed my lips to hers, just a bare taste, a need, a want, and when I pulled away, I cursed again.

"Fuck. That was a mistake."

My chest heaved as I stared at her, as every moment of this past weekend, hell, of these past months where I had been near her—a slight touch, a soft caress, a glare, a growl—went through my mind. Everything that had happened between us that I had purposely ignored hit me for the first time, the second time, every time.

And I couldn't focus.

"A mistake? No, for the first time," she whispered,

before she lowered her head, took a deep breath. "For the first time it wasn't a mistake."

I blinked at her, frowning. "What the hell are you talking about, Lake?"

"Why can't this just be my own choice? Why can't I choose you in this moment? Why does it have to be complicated? Why can't we just have tonight without everybody taking it away and freaking out? Because I see the way you watch me."

"Lake."

"It's the same way that I watch you. Why are we acting like this? Why are we freaking out and you wanting to run away because you kissed me? Just like I ran away because you stood up for me. Why can't we just have this moment?"

"Are you talking about what I think you're talking about right now?"

My hands were on her shoulders, gently caressing her soft skin before I even realized it. Because damn it, I *had* thought of this moment. Far too many times over the past years.

I had done my best not to think of her. Not to think of this, and yet how could I not? When she was so damn beautiful that she took my breath away, and it was hard to think, hard to breathe. She didn't seem to want to pull away in this moment. Didn't seem to want to run away from me.

"You have to be sure, Lake."

"I'm sure in most of my life. I make decisions and I stand by them, and I believe in them. And yet for the entire time I've known you I've done my best not to think of you. We fight so much. Do you ever wonder why?"

I snorted, gently brushing my fingers along her cheek. She leaned into it, and I swallowed hard.

"I know why. Because it's easier to fight than to do anything else."

"This won't be a mistake. Because we won't let it."

And I had to hope to hell that was the truth.

I lowered my head and brushed my lips against hers, and I was lost.

I slid my fingers along her shoulders again and she moaned into me. This was stupid. Beyond idiotic, but I didn't care right then. I wanted more. To do this again and to not stop.

We would think about what this meant later. If it meant anything. But right then and there, if this was what she wanted, then I would let myself ignore the reasons we shouldn't and do what I wanted as well.

"Nick," she whispered as I slid my lips down her jaw over her neck.

I knew her neck was sensitive, and not just in the way she moaned. But from the way she had stiffened along my touch when I had put her necklace on, and I swallowed hard.

"Is this okay?" I asked.

"Yes. I trust you, Nick." She looked up at me, wide-eyed and serious, and I nodded.

"Good." I kissed her again, just that one phrase, trust echoing within me.

"If you're sure," I whispered again before I slowly undid the clasp on her necklace, my fingers gently brushing her skin. She shivered, as if the touch was good for her, and I took that as a win. We continued to kiss, both of us knowing this was insane. Or at least that's what I figured. For all I knew this was what she wanted, what she had been thinking of forever. Then again, this was what I had been thinking of. Maybe I wasn't losing my mind. Maybe this was okay.

She groaned against me, and then we slowly walked towards the bedroom.

I grinned at the king-size bed, then looked down at her as she raised a brow.

"What's so funny?" she asked, looking like the Lake that I knew. This was all new and scary and different, and yet, some things were the same. Like this being Lake.

I needed to get out of my head. I was good at this. At sex and seduction. I needed to remember that.

"Just thinking about the fact that this might be the first time I actually get to sleep in this bed."

She shoved at my shoulder gently and rolled her eyes.

"You could have done so this whole time."

I raised a brow. "How would I have when I would have wanted to wake up in the middle of the night and see how wet you were. To press myself against you, to rock along your body, just so you could see how hard I was every time you are around."

Her eyes widened. "Seriously?"

I laughed, kissed her lips, then her shoulder, then her neck. "Do you know how hard it is to hide morning wood? And it's not just morning. You show up in those flowy pants and that top that makes your breasts look perky, and my cock presses against my jeans. I was here to be your friend, to be your stand-in so people didn't ask questions, and it was all I could do not to get a hard-on every time you walked into a room."

That was probably too honest. Too bare. But it wasn't like I could take back the words now.

Her eyes widened, then she slowly undid my tie, then the buttons of my shirt. I watched her work, taking her sweet time because I knew as soon as this moment ended, the bubble would burst and there'd be no going back to normal.

Not that I knew what normal was anyway.

"I've thought about you, too, you know. Even when I shouldn't. Maybe that's a problem. But one we can rectify right now."

I took off my shirt, let it drop to the floor. And as soon as my hands were at my belt, she stepped back and undid the ties on the sides of her dress. I had no idea that it had only been staying up by those single ties, or I would have had a problem for the entire evening thinking about her. Because as soon as she shifted her hips slightly, the dress fell to her feet, pooling on the floor.

I groaned at the sight of her in a tiny bra with no straps, barely any lace at all, and an even tinier set of panties.

"You're going to kill me."

"I had to worry about lines under this dress. But I couldn't go naked with you around. At least naked under this dress. When you touched my neck earlier? When you put on this necklace, my breath caught, and it was hard for me to even breathe. And my panties got wet just thinking of it."

I groaned.

"We are insane."

"Maybe. But at least we can be insane together right now."

"Deal." And then my mouth was on hers again,

and my hands were sliding through her hair. I couldn't be rough, not with Lake. Not with who she had been and what we were together. Because she was my friend, and I knew she had been through hell. And that's when I froze.

"What?" she asked, looking up at me.

"I don't want to hurt you."

"You're not going to hurt me."

I shook my head. "Lake. Is this the first time since…" I asked, breaking the moment.

"Oh, Nick." She shook her head. "Yes, but I'm okay. He didn't hurt me like that. And you're not going to either. I promise. I want this. And if I don't for any reason, if something changes, I'll let you know, and I trust you with everything that I have. I trust you to stop if I need to stop. So kiss me, okay? I don't want to be the wounded bird that I think you see when you look at me sometimes. I want to be the Lake that makes you laugh. I want to be the Lake that makes you come."

I groaned. "Okay then." I kissed her again, my hands wrapping around her.

I gently laid her on the bed, hovering over her after I pulled off my pants. I still wore my boxer briefs, not wanting to startle her too much. She writhed on the bed, still in her bra and panties, so I hovered over her, pressing a kiss to her collarbone, in between her breasts over her bra.

"Nick."

"Let me look at you. Taste you. You make it hard to want anything else."

She groaned as I slowly pulled down the cup of her bra, exposing her pale pink nipple. I blew cool air over it and it pebbled, looking sexy as fuck. And when I leaned down to suck her nipple into my mouth, she arched into me.

"Nick."

"So beautiful. Soft." I did the same thing to her other breast, and both of us groaned, her taste a sweet sin that was never going to forget.

She moved gently, arching her back so she could undo the clasp of her bra, and I tossed it to the floor, looking down at her in her goddess form.

"You're so fucking beautiful."

"You're making it hard to breathe."

I grinned, then went back down to play with her breasts, kneading and sucking until she was writhing under me, my thigh between her legs as she rode me. I could feel her heat and wetness through her panties, so when I slid my hand down between her legs, she sucked in a breath and froze.

I did the same, looking down at her. "Okay?"

She nodded. "I'm okay. I just didn't realize I was already on a trigger."

I laughed. "Well then. Let's see what I can do."

I met that honey-brown gaze of hers and slowly slid my hand underneath her panties, my middle finger sliding over her clit.

She hummed, her mouth parting as I gently rubbed small circles over her, once, twice, her breaths coming in sweet pants as I slowly slid my fingers over her wetness, spreading her folds. She was small, tight, and when I gently inserted one finger, she clamped around me, her whole body rolling in a moan.

So close. So close. I gently prodded her entrance, inserting another finger, watching the way her entire body flushed. And when I slid my thumb over her clit, rocking to the motion as I fingered her, she came.

The sweet ecstasy of sensation nearly made me come in my briefs.

She rolled her hips, riding my hand, when she finally came down, I grinned, looking down at her.

"Beautiful."

And then she was reaching for me, sliding her hand underneath the band of my boxer briefs, taking me in hand.

I groaned and she smiled up at me, fisting me.

"Be careful. You do that too much, we're not going to have much fun after."

"I think I can handle that." She sat up as I kneeled over her and kissed me.

I deepened the kiss, wrapping my arm around her,

as she worked me in her hand, her fist tightening with each movement.

She was so damn sexy it was hard to breathe, but it didn't matter. This was Lake. My Lake. If only for a moment. And it might be a mistake. Such a big mistake that it would change everything but I didn't care in that moment. It was as if we had been waiting for this for eons, and finally I was letting those wet dreams of mine, those errant thoughts that I wouldn't give any consideration to previously, come forward.

It didn't matter that we would walk away in the morning and never talk about this again. Because with her holding me in that small hand of hers, it was all I could do not to keep thrusting, and to want more.

"Nick. I don't have a condom," she said after a moment, and she stilled her hand on my dick, my hand between her legs.

I cursed under my breath, then kissed her hard on the mouth. "I've got one in my bag."

She narrowed her gaze at me, and I laughed outright.

"First, I always have one in my bag, because you never know. Second, don't get mad; without it, we wouldn't be continuing."

"Go get it. And I'm going to have to add condoms to my bag for the future."

I growled at her, kissed her hard, then practically ran to my bag for a condom.

My dick bobbed against my stomach, and I shucked off my boxer briefs, and ran back. I caught the panties as she threw them at me, rolled my eyes, and threw them over my shoulder before I came back and practically pounced on top of her.

She laughed with me, as I wondered how I could laugh in this situation.

I was about to make love with Lake fucking Montgomery. How the hell had that happened? And why the hell did this seem like exactly what we should be doing?

I rolled the condom over my length before I positioned myself between her legs.

"Tell me when to stop."

"I don't think I'm going to do that," she whispered, and I kissed her hard, before I sank deep inside her. Her pussy clenched along my cock, tight and hot and wet.

She moaned against me, wrapping her legs around my waist, before I was finally fully seated, and we both shook, our bodies sweat-slick.

"Dear God. I can't, I'm so full. How can…"

I smiled against her lips, kissed her again.

"Ready for me to move?"

"I think I'm ready to come right now," she whispered, so I kissed her again, and moved.

She did indeed come around my cock, her orgasm rolling to the point that I nearly came, and I rocked my hips, slowly working in and out of her. I wouldn't go fast, wouldn't go hard, just slowly so I could feel her. So I could stretch out this moment because I knew there wouldn't be another. Not after now. Not after everything had changed.

When she looked up at me, her eyes wide, I kissed her again and nodded.

"It's okay, Lake. I'm here."

I wiped away her tears, because I knew they weren't for me, but for her. At least I had to hope. And when she held me, her hands sliding down my back, I came, shaking, as I crushed my mouth to hers, afraid I'd say something wrong. Afraid I'd say something at all.

Because I had just done the one thing I had been thinking about for years.

The one thing I had always known I couldn't.

I had just slept with my friend, my sometimes enemy, and the one woman who had been off limits for most of my life.

And there was no going back.

Chapter 9

Lake

WHEN MORNING BROKE, THE SUN SLIDING THROUGH the shades, I slowly opened my eyes and wondered which reality I'd stepped into.

The reality where things made sense, where I hadn't just had sex with one of my best friends—who I fought with more often than not. Or the one where I seemed to currently reside.

I lay in a comfortable king-size bed, the duvet over us both, the sheets tangled on the floor, two pillows on the ground, another one shared by us.

After the first time, when he had been so sweet and

gentle, he lowered his body and licked and sucked me into completion once more before he found his final condom, one I was deeply grateful for, and I rode him, breasts bouncing, him tugging on my hair, me scratching down his chest.

I had cried at first, not because of who he was or who I was, but because of the moment in general.

It had just felt so full, so *everything*. And that was something I had to deal with. That I cried as he had sunk deep inside me, and he wiped my tears as if it hadn't bothered him in the slightest.

I was standing in the remnants of who I once was, and now I lay in his arms, his deep breaths warm against the back of my neck. He had one hand around my body, over my stomach, between my breasts, as he cupped me. Just one breast, the other resting on his forearm, as if this was the most natural pose in the world. And maybe it was. Maybe it could be with him.

Or maybe I was losing my mind.

This weekend had been a whirlwind.

Ned hadn't truly harmed me, he had threatened to, and Nick took care of it. If I made it a bigger deal, it would be something I might have to worry about later, and I didn't want to. I didn't want to be the center of another incident where nothing could be done because he technically hadn't *done* anything. He wouldn't be kicked out of the event, and they would continue to praise him for being amazing. So I wouldn't say anything. At least not yet.

Perhaps I would do what all women did in business situations and warn other women. It was our secret code that wasn't so secret.

But I didn't want to think about that man. I didn't want to think about the fact that the first time I had been with someone since Zach was with Nick of all people. Because I had thought about this before. About the maybes. Just like any girl who looked up to her older cousin and his best friend. Because Leif's best friend had always made me swoon, even when we butted heads.

Nick moved, grunting as he curled even more around me, all protective like, and I pressed my lips together.

Well shit. Shit shit shit.

I was all warm and happy and sore and I hadn't had a panic attack.

Last night, well wrapped up in him, I was feeling every moment and inch of him and us. I hadn't panicked in the slightest. I lived in the moment and said what I wanted—and I had gotten it.

I hadn't panicked or had to count to ten or felt like I was losing my mind.

I pressed my lips together and figured my therapist would call that progress.

I might have to call that a delusion.

He grunted again, still sleeping, but when his hand lowered, his face pressed against the back of my neck, I knew I needed to get up. We had a flight to catch and a lot of thinking to do.

Because as soon as we left this bed, the moment would be broken. Then again, perhaps it was already broken.

I gently rolled out of bed, holding back a smile as he rolled to the center of the bed over the warm spot I had made and laid face down like a starfish. He was a bed hog.

Was that something I was supposed to know? That one of my best friends was such a bed hog that he would immediately roll over and take as much space as he could.

I took a quick shower because I could smell him on my skin and I wouldn't be able to function on an airplane or travel or deal with anything else if I could. I washed my hair, annoyed with myself for not even bothering to take off my makeup last night or brushing out my hair before bed. I looked a mess, but I didn't care. I would be smooth and glowy and dewy and all ready for the day. When he woke up I wouldn't look as if my world had been irreparably altered.

I didn't bother to blow-dry my hair. Instead, I put it into a semi-complicated bun along with a headband and called it a day. I did a quick makeup session, no foundation, but some powder, brightener, and three coats of mascara. That would be my shield for the day, along with sunglasses, lip gloss, and the air of knowing what I was doing. Even if it was all a lie.

We had mostly packed the day before, but I finished packing, trying to be as quiet as possible. We still had some time, and I wanted him to sleep. This was his first time being able to sleep in a bed for this entire trip. He deserved it.

He deserved many things.

And I wasn't going to think too much about that statement.

He groaned and I looked over as he sat in the bed, running his hands over his hair. I watched the muscles in his arms and chest move, noticed that the sheet barely covered him, and I could see his bare hip.

I swallowed hard and then moved back to the suitcase.

"I'm just packing, but the shower's all yours."

"Okay."

That was it, that's all he said, until I heard him groan again, get out of bed, and walk—presumably naked—to the bathroom. I hadn't looked, and it had taken all of my patience and willpower to do so.

I heard the shower going and ignored the image in

my head of him wet and slick and rubbing soap all over.

We were never going to do this again. I'd had a moment of delusions, and it wasn't going to happen again.

And yet, why did I feel like I was losing my mind?

By the time he was out of the shower, I was already packed and ordering us breakfast.

"They have this English muffin thing to-go that I ordered, and we get free breakfast with the room every day, so that's why I went all out."

"No problem," he mumbled, and I looked over to see him dressed in jeans and a T-shirt that clung to his muscles, but he was still barefoot.

I swallowed hard, wondering why things were so weird now?

Oh yes, because the night before he pounded you into the mattress, remember?

Hard and fast, and soft and slow. It had felt like perfection, and I came more than once. Something I had never done before.

I'd had great sex before, but I'd never had sex with Nick before. And somehow that was even better than anything else, and I had no idea how I was supposed to go back to being normal.

"Sounds good. I'm all ready to go."

"Okay, good."

He looked at me then, studied my face, before he shook his head and went back to the bathroom to presumably pick something up.

The staff came with our breakfast, and we called the bellhop to get our bags, and suddenly I was looking at a cold English muffin in my hand in the back of an SUV on our ride back to the airport. Nick ate his like nothing mattered or had happened the night before, and maybe that was fine. Maybe I just needed to get over myself.

He gave me a look, and I took a bite of my sandwich, not wanting him to get grumpy at me for not eating. He tended to do that at the shop, so I wouldn't give him a reason to now.

Oh God, I was going to have to see him at the shop, and everywhere else. I had wanted a night with him, a moment. Just to be. And now I didn't know what to say. I was so awkward at this.

But he wasn't helping by being his broody silent self. While it might be hot in other times, right now it just made me nervous.

We barely spoke in the car, or in the airport or on the plane. When we did speak it was about nothing important, and we sure as hell hadn't brought up what had happened between us. This was so wrong, and we had messed things up. And I didn't know how to fix it.

When he pulled into my driveway to drop me off, I sighed and got my bags.

"So, are we going to talk about it?" he asked. I jumped, not realizing that he was standing right behind me, and nearly fell.

"No? Maybe? How? We're adults. We can do this. We can still be friends."

That was the worst thing to say. I didn't want to just be friends. I should have had an idea of something to say. I'd had this entire traveling day, and yet nothing had come to me because I was so nervous. Because I didn't know *what* I wanted, so how was I supposed to make things better?

"Really?" He let out a laugh that once again did things to me I didn't want to think about.

"We're business partners. Leif calls me brother. That makes us family doesn't it?" he asked, sarcasm drenching his tone.

I shuddered. "No, it doesn't."

Hurt crossed his face, and I backpedaled. "I mean, we're not family. Not in that weird banjo-playing way. Not after last night."

He laughed, before he sobered up. "So I didn't hurt you?" he asked, his voice soft.

All the tension from before slid out of me, even as I moved forward. "Of course not. We had consensual sex." Look at me sounding like an adult who knew what I was doing. It couldn't be further from the truth.

"We fight all the time. And we're friends. And I just, I don't want to hurt our group. Our people."

I don't want to hurt you.

He nodded at me, his jaw tightening.

"You're right. We wouldn't want to hurt our people." And with that, he handed me my suitcases, leaving me beside my driveway before he got in his SUV and backed out. He didn't move, though, and I knew he wanted to wait for me to go inside.

But what was I supposed to say? What was I supposed to do?

So I waved at him like an awkward idiot and pulled my suitcases into the house, locking myself inside.

Where apparently I would be safe.

And away from Nick.

I heard the SUV drive off, and I let out a breath.

I'd made a mistake.

With him just then?

Or with my actions in general.

Knowing I didn't have time to wallow, because my world couldn't just be about my feelings, I rolled my suitcases back to my bedroom so I could unpack. My siblings always called my ability to unpack right when I got home a sign of being insane, or at least something that a monster would do, but I knew they were just joking. And I couldn't just have suitcases lying around my house.

I began to unpack when my phone rang. I looked down at the readout and froze.

It wasn't Nick. He wasn't calling to check in or make sure I was okay or to talk about what happened and what we should do about it.

But I really wished it was.

I ignored Zach's call and quickly sent off an email to my contact at the police department, telling them that Zach had called again. There was nothing they could do, as Zach wasn't harassing me. Not in the eyes of the law.

But I would keep up. Keep everything documented, and I wouldn't cry. Even though I really wanted to.

I finished unpacking and started to get things ready for the next day. I had meetings, and phone calls, and countless other things to do. I wanted to talk with Susanna and work on the school and other charities. I had an entire life that didn't revolve around love and sex and heat and mistakes. I just had to remember that.

My phone buzzed again and I froze, hoping it was Nick. And once again it wasn't. It thankfully also wasn't Zach.

Diana's name filled the screen and I answered, a small smile on my lips.

"Hello, Diana. I was just thinking about our meeting for tomorrow."

"Me too. I know we were planning lunch at your place, but how about we try the café next to my house?"

I smiled and nodded, even though she couldn't see me. "That's perfect. I'll schedule that in and make sure everyone knows."

"Great, I know it's last minute, but it just came to me. Honestly, it's the best idea."

We talked a few more minutes about upcoming things, and when I hung up, I sat on my couch, pressed my face to my knees, and wanted to cry. Because I couldn't focus, couldn't do anything. I was such a mess.

And I had only myself to blame.

Chapter 10

Nick

"Thank you so much. Seriously. I am in awe and so grateful." Candace hugged me tightly before waving and skipping out of the shop, talking a mile a minute with her friends.

I shook my head as both Leo and Leif looked at me, grins on their faces.

"I'm pretty sure she enjoyed that tattoo," Leo teased.

I scowled. "Shut up."

"I'm just saying. She flirted with you the entire time, and you didn't say a damn thing back."

"Because I was working."

"This is the second time she's been here, and you were a little more receptive the first time. What's changed?" Leo asked, staring at me.

Damn the man being far too perceptive for his own good. And the real problem was that Leif was even more so. That was the problem when you worked with your friends. They saw through you and knew your secrets even before you were aware of them. But it wasn't like I was going to tell the men in this room what had happened.

In the week since we had gotten back, I'd thrown myself into work, and just regular life things, without focusing on what the hell happened with Lake.

I should probably call her, should have probably said something, but she wanted to just remain friends. Coworkers. So we wouldn't hurt one another or our friends. Because apparently sleeping together ruined the dynamic completely. And while part of me probably would've agreed with that, I hadn't liked the fact that she's the one who'd said it.

Call me selfish, but fuck it. I didn't want to hear it.

Ashamed of me? Fine. I didn't need her anyway.

The fact that I was oddly glad and pissed off that she hadn't shown up at the shop when I had been there since, notwithstanding. I wasn't going to think about that. Because that would make things too important.

"So you're not going to hit on her back? I thought you were well on your way to before. My mistake."

I looked at my friend and fellow tattoo artist. Leo was a good man, a great artist, and even more sarcastic than I was. That was saying something.

"When are you going to get out there and actually start hitting back on any of the women that hit on you in here?"

"When it clicks of course. And, the only reason I said anything this time is because I thought you were reciprocating during her first session. That hot and cold thing must have confused the fuck out of her."

I shook my head, cleaning up my station.

"You know what? I'm just here to do a job."

"I would believe that if you weren't scowling," Leif said as he studied my face.

"You done trying to psychoanalyze me? We've got things to do."

I couldn't stop thinking about the last week. The fact that I hadn't seen her but I needed to talk to her, but I knew she didn't want to. And there wasn't any way in hell I was going to talk about it with anyone else. It wasn't their business, and as soon as it became their business, things would get more fucked up than they already were. And there was no way that I was going to be part of that.

I finished cleaning up as Leo and Leif laughed

about something, thankfully nothing to do with me. They were cleaning up and getting ready for their next appointments, when the bell above the door chimed and I looked up.

It felt as if time had frozen, and everything burned around me.

I couldn't focus, couldn't breathe. This wasn't happening. This couldn't be happening with her. In this moment. With that person.

Because it wasn't Lake at the door. I really wished it was Lake at the door.

"Nick. I'm sorry to bother you, but I have a few things for you, and I wanted to talk."

There was such pain and hope in her eyes, such worry and trepidation.

And I didn't blame my mother one bit for that.

"I can't do that. You need to go."

"Nick."

Leif stood up and frowned, looking between us. Considering he had gone through something similar with his birth mother's former boyfriend, I didn't blame him.

"I really can't do this right now. You're going to have to go."

"I understand. I just have a few things of your father's and your grandfather's. And I know I should probably have just sent them to you. But I was selfish and wanted to see you."

"I'm not doing this right now. Please go."

She nodded, then set down a small key on the front table.

"It's a safety deposit box. If you want it. None of my stuff's in there. It's your history. Not mine."

And as she turned to go, I saw the other woman in the doorway and wanted to scream.

But, of course, I couldn't.

My mother murmured something to Lake I didn't hear, and then she was gone.

"Nick," Leif called out, and I held up my hand.

"I need a minute," I muttered under my breath, then pushed past Lake. I couldn't talk to her. I couldn't talk to anyone.

Because I didn't hate my mother. I couldn't. But I didn't have to like her either. And that was the problem.

"Nick!" Lake called after me, but I kept going.

I walked past the end of the building, then towards the small park in the back. It was only a couple of trees and a little bench. It wasn't much, but it was ours. I knew that Brooke and Lake wanted to build something else, to buy this patch of land and make it even better. Just like we wanted one of the Montgomerys to open up a café in our small little strip mall; somehow they were going to take over, and I was going to go along for the ride. That is, if I fucking got out of my head.

"Nick." Lake put her hand on my back and I stiffened. I couldn't do much else. Because it was Lake. And just like Leif, I would tell her everything. Her touch comforting in a way it hadn't been before. Because things had changed despite the fact that I had told myself they hadn't. They had altered in a way that there would be no changing who we were to each other.

"That was my mom."

I turned to her, her eyes were wide, and she looked so fucking beautiful it was hard to breathe. But I was used to that happening around Lake.

"You have her eyes. From what I saw of them."

I let out a hollow laugh. "I look just like my dad. Did I ever tell you he was a firefighter?"

She nodded, reached out, and held my hand. I looked down at her small hand in my larger one and wondered how we had ever fit. Even if for a night, but here we were, and I wasn't sure why I should hold back. So I wouldn't.

"My mom was the best fucking mom until my dad died. I was ten. He died in a fire—he went in to save a family, and he didn't come out again. It happens. That's what they tell you as firefighters' families. They give you a shitty insurance payout, a couple of slaps on the back, then they tell you that they're going to be there for you forever. Only sometimes it doesn't work out that way."

"Nick, you don't have to go into this if you don't want to."

"No. Why not? You got to see the embarrassment that was my past in full force, why shouldn't you know all of it?" I let out a breath as she stared at me. But she didn't walk away. She didn't pull away.

"Some stations would've stayed by us. Would've invited us to all the cookouts and raised us like their own. Our station didn't do that. The chief retired after my dad died, and he moved away. Be near his grand-kids I guess. At least that's what Mom said. The other guys moved on or were I guess worried that one day it would be them. So they didn't reach out. Other stations would have. My dad's didn't. And I think that's what broke my mom a bit."

Lake looked at me and I reached out, pushed her hair from her face. Her skin was so soft, and I knew I shouldn't touch her, but I craved it.

"My mom never hit me. Didn't beat me or really yell at me. She just checked out. Just like the station. She gave up. She worked the hours that she needed to. Nothing more, nothing less, which, you know, is fine. But she didn't come to my school functions, didn't watch me play sports. She didn't come to parent-teacher conferences, she didn't fucking care. Leif's parents cared. They were the ones that helped."

"I'm sorry. I knew you were there a lot. That's why we became friends. At least at first. But I didn't know."

"Leif did, his parents did. Nobody else needed to. My mom didn't abuse me. She just fucking forgot about me. Decided that she was done being a mom. One day she got sad enough that she looked at me and said that I was too much of my dad. That she saw me and remembered the fact that my dad worked his ass off and was always away from us. That no matter what we did, he was with his station, never us. The same station that gave up on us. So yeah, she didn't care anymore. That small stipend from the insurance paid for the house, and part of my school. I got loans and worked my ass off for the rest. I bought into this company. Did all of it on my own. Mom didn't even check in on me. Didn't even notice when I moved out. When I moved in with Leif, and then with a couple of other guys when Leif went to Europe. She didn't care. And then when she finally woke up, I guess, she decided to come here and talk to me. But what am I supposed to do?"

"Do you want to fix it with your mom? You don't have to. My birth parents are gone. I would love to be able to talk to them and ask them why. To show them who I am now. But in the end, Liam and Arden are my real parents. They love me. And Uncle Austin and Aunt Sierra love you. But do you want to fix it with your mom?"

"No. I just want to yell and scream and tell her that even though she never physically abused me, she forgot me. She fucking *forgot* me. I don't know what to do. I want to do something, and there's just so much in me, so whatever I end up doing is probably going to be fucking wrong."

Lake was standing so close to me I couldn't breathe, I couldn't focus, and when she looked up at me, I knew I was going to make a mistake.

"So I'm just going to do this," I whispered, as she hugged me and I sucked in a breath and tried not to move. Tried not to do anything. I didn't want to break this moment. Because Lake was holding me, and I was holding her back, but when she kissed my jaw, I broke.

I kissed her hard and fast on the mouth, needing her. She was everything, my past, my present, but I wasn't going to call her my future. Not when all I could focus on was her taste.

"Oh fuck," she whispered against my lips, and I grinned down at her.

"Yeah. Fuck."

She trailed her fingers along my jaw, frowning at me. "Before, when you asked if we were going to talk about it, I said I was worried about hurting people." I froze, wondering why the fuck she wanted to talk about that now. "I meant our friends, yes, but I don't want to hurt you. I like you, Nick. And if I mess this up, I don't want it to hurt you. So I want us to be cognizant of that as we try to figure out what the hell we're doing."

"Oh." Well, now I felt like shit. Because she hadn't wanted to hurt me, and there I was, blowing things out of proportion. Just like I'd just done with my mom. Something I was damn good at.

I rubbed my thumb along her lips, and she stared at me, wide-eyed.

"I don't want to hurt you either," I whispered.

"So what are we doing? Are we really doing this?"

I smiled, kissed her softly, knowing I was making a damn mistake but not caring.

"*Apparently*."

"Oh fuck." I whirled and stared at my best friend. Leif Montgomery stood there, wide-eyed, staring between us.

"Um."

Lake gripped my hand, I stared at my best friend, and knew I was in deep shit.

Chapter 11

Lake

MY HEART RACED, AND I TOLD MYSELF THAT everything would be okay. That this was a dream. It wasn't a nightmare, maybe an anxiety-filled dream, but not a nightmare.

"I have questions." Leif stared at us, wide-eyed and yet…not surprised.

I assumed my cousin had questions, considering he had just seen his best friend kissing me in the park behind our shop.

Probably not the most discreet place, but I hadn't been thinking about anyone but Nick.

And we still hadn't finished our conversation. Because what did that kiss mean?

"Seriously. Questions."

"It's not what you think," I blurted at the same time as Nick said, "It's not like that."

Hurt sliced against my heart, even though I had just said something similar, and I gave him a look. He raised a brow before he rolled his eyes.

Then he opened his mouth to speak, but I held up my hand. No, Leif was my cousin, and Nick and I needed to focus on exactly what was going on between us and not worry about the family, which wasn't always easy.

"Please go. Nick and I need to finish our conversation."

Nick's lips twitched, and I sucked in a breath.

"Seriously, what the fuck is going on?"

I narrowed my gaze, even as Nick reached out and gripped my hand to give it a squeeze. My cousin noticed the action and narrowed his gaze. He didn't look angry, just bewildered. And honestly, I didn't blame him. All that Nick and I ever did these days was fight. At least in front of everyone else. Behind closed doors? That was something different. That was something the two of us needed to talk about. Alone.

Leif might be confused, but I wasn't just going to

blurt out what I was thinking in front of him. Especially when I wasn't even sure what that was.

"I love you, Leif, but don't be a jerk right now, okay?"

"You're right," Leif said as he looked between us, his eyes wide. He threw his hands up in the air. "I know it's not my business. But I love you both. So if you need to talk with me? Go for it. I'm here. Same with Brooke, I bet. Make that happen because, dude. This was not what I was expecting." He waved his hands between us. "I mean, you guys fight, but I didn't think you guys *fought*." He emphasized the word fought, and I held back a laugh.

"Are you done freaking out?" Nick asked, his voice low.

"I'm not quite sure," Leif answered. "Because you sure as hell know that I'm not going to be the only one that freaks out."

"Keep this to yourself," I said quickly. I looked at Nick. "Not because I'm ashamed. I'm not."

His lips twitched. "I figured. You're never ashamed of anything that you do."

I blushed and Leif cleared his throat. "Seriously. So many questions, but I kind of don't want any details. So I'm just going to let whatever this is be, and I'm going back to work. Nick, you have a client in two hours, and I know you wanted to go over paperwork.

Lake, I assume you're going to want to do the same. Just don't dirty up the office."

Nick flipped him off as I scowled.

"Grow up."

"What? I've made out with Brooke in that office. It's a nice office."

I cringed. "Seriously? That's a shared space."

"We didn't have sex in the office. My God. You know that Sebastian's made out with Marley in there, too, right?" Leif asked.

"That much I knew. It's a good place for privacy these days for that couple."

I looked between them, aghast. "I will not make out with Nick in the office."

"Ever, or just like today?" Nick asked, his eyes filled with laughter, as Leif snorted.

I looked between them, utterly bewildered. "First off, I need a minute. And you and I need to talk." I looked at my cousin. "Go away."

"That's not very nice, cousin."

"Really?" I growled, a real growl, just like Nick often did.

"Nice. A little more guttural next time," Nick teased as Leif beamed.

This is how it always was between us. It was us three amigos against the world, taking turns on who we would gang up on. Apparently this time it was me.

And I still had no idea what I was doing with Nick. Because I wanted him to kiss me again, but if we screwed this up? It would ruin this dynamic. It was already different now, and how was I supposed to think?

Nick seemed to sense that my emotions were going off the rails, so he gestured towards Leif.

"I'm going to take Lake out to lunch. We need to talk."

"What?" I asked.

"I'm hungry, pissed off, and can't deal. So let's go eat."

Leif looked between us, shrugged, waved, and headed back into the shop.

"Keep this between us," I called out.

"Not going to lie to Brooke," he said over his shoulder before he jogged back. I just stared at Nick.

"You want to eat right now?"

"There's a lot of things I want to do right now, but eating sounds good."

Why did I feel like he wasn't talking about food? But I wasn't going to let my mind wander.

"Like, on a date?" I blurted, wondering why that was the first thing that came to mind.

Nick smiled and finally looked relaxed. Because this wasn't just about me and him, it was about his mom too. Everything. And I didn't know how to make it better, or even if I should. But I wanted to be with him. Somehow.

"Yeah, Lake. Let's call it a date."

And crap.

"Where are we going?" I asked, feeling as though I was having an out of body experience.

"Where do you want to go?" I saw the tension in his shoulders, the way his jaw tightened. I knew he wasn't okay. And it probably had nothing to do with Leif, and maybe not even me. This was something deeper, so we would talk. Because above all else, he was my friend. Even if something might have just shifted.

"How about that café within walking distance?"

"Sure. I know you like that spinach salad they have."

I smiled. "I do. Although right now I could do with a big hearty sandwich with French bread."

He groaned. "Damn it, now I want French bread. And you know the best sandwiches and bread that they have are at your friend's place down in Denver."

I nodded as I walked beside him. We were both very careful not to touch, as if we knew this moment was important. Why did I feel so awkward? I wasn't new at dating or whatever this was. But I was new to this version of Nick.

"You don't have to stay away from me, you know.

I'm not going to jump you on the sidewalk. Not unless you ask nicely."

I nearly tripped over my own feet, reaching out to Nick's arm to keep me steady. He raised a brow and I rolled my eyes at him.

"You're trying to make me act the fool."

"I would say I wasn't trying, but that would make you feel as though I was actually calling you the fool. And you're not."

"So what am I?"

He looked down at me, his face impassive. "You're my friend Lake. Even if sometimes you annoy the fuck out of me."

I stared at him, my mouth open, before I threw my head back and laughed.

An older woman walked past us, glaring, but I ignored her. "Oh my God. Is that how you're going to hit on me?"

"I don't need to hit on you, Lake."

"Excuse me? No. If you want whatever 'this' to happen, you're going to have to work for it."

"Oh I can work for it. But I don't have to hit on you. I can just be myself. And you can be yourself. Maybe we can finally figure out what the fuck we're doing."

"Does this work on other women?"

"You're not other women, Lake."

Maybe some part of me should have taken that as a blow, considering I knew he saw more than his fair share of women. But not with the way that Nick said it. He meant something different. And I sort of hated the fact that I was melting.

"So you're not going to hit on me?"

"No. I can still make you swoon."

I pushed at his arm. "I do not swoon. And seriously? Are these real moves you're using?"

"I don't know yet. I don't know what the fuck I'm doing, Lake. But I'm hungry. Let's go eat."

"Okay, we can do that."

"Finally."

He took my hand and practically dragged me into the café.

I held back a laugh, because I knew he was annoyed about this whole situation too. This wasn't what I was used to, this Nick who wasn't sure of himself, and yet growling. But I think I liked it. And there was probably something wrong with me because of that.

"Okay then," he said as we sat down at a table, looking at the menu. "How'd that vampire thing go?"

I blinked up at him. "As in pointy teeth?"

He just stared at me. "You had a meeting with the vampire lady."

It took me a minute to realize what he was saying.

"The café. Oh, it's going great. It'll be up and running soon. I'm happy that I'm an investor. You're really going to like it."

"There's not real blood or anything, is there?"

"There's going to be no blood," I said with a laugh. "There will be drinks and blood bags. And random vampire-esque and goth-esque items."

"There will be a cheese plate though, right? You're a Montgomery. There needs to be a cheese plate."

I put my hand to my chest. "Of course there's going to be a cheese plate. Who do you think I am?"

"Well, it's the little things. We worry."

I smiled at him, and before I could say anything, the waitress was there, and we ordered two sandwiches on crusty French bread and iced teas.

"I'm surprised you didn't get a cheese plate for lunch now."

I put my hand over my stomach. "I thought about it. But I was craving the one down at our other café." I whispered that last part, and he bit back a smile.

"Your next goal in your world-takeover business is to find a person to come and build our favorite café next to the shop."

"I'll think about it. But I have a few other things in mind first."

"Are you talking about work now? Or something else."

I pressed my lips together as the waitress came back with our iced teas. Grateful, I gulped a good third of mine, while Nick just stared at me, shaking his head.

"What? I'm trying to remember what I was doing."

"How about you just talk to me."

"I was going to say the same to you."

He looked at me, then shook his head. "I don't want to talk about my mom. Or anyone else right now."

"What are we doing then?" I asked, and he rolled his eyes.

"For fuck's sake, I hate that question."

My lips twitched. "Well, it's a good question."

"Maybe. But do we need a label? It's been forty-five minutes."

He sounded so grumpy, and I liked it. There was seriously something wrong with me.

"Okay. No labels. We'll just be. So I guess this means we get to eat cheese and sandwiches and go out together, and then what?"

"And we don't hide whatever this is."

I looked at him. "I would never want to hide this. I also don't want the rest of our family to be in the middle of the situation at all times."

"So we're in a situation?"

I flipped him off discreetly and he just snorted.

"Sorry. Sorry."

"You better be. But I don't want our family to have an opinion. Or at least one that's going to shade everything."

"See. You said it right there. Our family. 'Cause yeah, Leif is family."

"So we figure things out. No labels, no interruptions. And you're allowed to growl."

He looked at me and laughed, looking far too sexy for his own damn good.

Then he leaned across the table and kissed me hard on the mouth. I blushed, ducking my head.

"Thank you. I will. I like spending time with you. I like seeing your mind work. I like going out to dinner with you when we talk about random shit that we see around us. I like the fact that when you're worried about work that you actually tell me things. At least, we used to. So let's keep doing that. And every once in a while, I'm going to kiss you."

Damn it. It was getting really hard not to freak out when he spoke like that. Because he was amazing. He was great. And he got me.

And I hated it. Because I didn't want him to get me. Or maybe that was the problem. Maybe I wanted him to get me. What exactly would that mean?

"You're thinking too much again."

"Maybe. Or maybe I'm not thinking enough."

He shook his head. "No. Far too much. We'll just

be. And if this fades, you don't look at me like I'm a horrible person. And I won't be a horrible person. And you don't stay away from your family because you're afraid of hurting me."

I looked at him, the kick to the gut unexpected.

"I wouldn't."

"I don't want you to lose your family because you're worried about me."

"I was just thinking I don't want you to lose this family because you're worried about me."

"So we don't worry. And we don't mess this up."

And when the waitress handed us our sandwiches, Nick took my hand and kissed my palm. I swallowed hard, my emotions a little too much.

Because this had come out of left field, even though truly it hadn't if I looked back hard enough.

I couldn't mess this up.

Only, I had this horrible worry that I would.

I refused to let him get hurt.

No matter if my heart broke along the way.

Chapter 12

Nick

"I CAN'T BELIEVE YOU TALKED ME INTO THIS," I SAID AS I glared over at Leif.

Leif shrugged and pointed at the windmill. "You know what to do. Just try to get it in the hole."

"That's what she said," Noah and Leo said at the same time, and as the two high-fived each other, I rolled my eyes.

"Really?" I asked Riley.

Leif shrugged. "You're just upset because you didn't say it first."

That made my lips twitch. "Maybe. I do not miniature golf."

"I'm going to have to disagree with that," Leo put in. "You are indeed here and miniature golfing."

I frowned. "First bowling, now miniature golfing. Why can't we just go to a sports bar and watch some sporting activity?"

Noah snorted. "Oh, good. That sounds well-intentioned and detailed. We're here because it sounded fun when I was about three beers in and laughing, and now here we are."

I shook my head. "Sebastian can't come?" I asked Leif.

He shook his head. "Nope. Marley had a sonogram today, then he had an evening class, and now I know they're both working on homework."

"He worked this morning in the shop going over a few things with us. That's a whole lot on his plate."

Leif nodded. "And it's only going to get worse when the baby comes. But he can do it. And it's not like he's alone. He's got the entire Montgomery brood on his side."

That made my lips curl up into a smile. "I suppose that is true. There are a few of you."

"And they're all in mourning because Marley is no longer allowed to have soft cheeses."

I looked at Leif and Noah, aghast, and the two Montgomerys bowed their heads in silence.

"So let me get this straight—when you marry or breed into the Montgomery family, does your love of cheese just show up? Or do you have to like, go through a whole class?"

"I don't know. I used to think it was genetic, but then people marrying in had cheese addictions. I think it's just subtle mind manipulation. You don't realize it until suddenly you are in love with cheese and planning your own cheese board."

Leif shook his head. "And, you have to be careful what you call charcuterie because that is cured meats, not a cheese board. There is a difference."

I looked at Leo who just shrugged. "Don't ask me, bro. They're the ones that scare me."

"We shouldn't scare you. That much."

I narrowed my eyes at Noah and shrugged. "Okay, let me try not to hit this stupid windmill."

"Wait till you get to the pirate ship. That's when it gets tricky."

I paused and stared at the other man. "How many times have you played here?"

"It's a good place to take a girl. At least when we were in high school. You can't get into some clubs, so you come here and wrap your arms around her as you're trying to show her exactly how to aim."

He wiggled his brows and I rolled my eyes.

"Oh, that's nice. So glad that I'm here to learn all

this."

"Well, you can try it out with my cousin now," Leif teased, and Leo and Noah just grinned.

I narrowed my gaze at my best friend.

"Really?"

"It's fine. I'm not going to say anything."

"You said something."

"We thought, but weren't sure. This is good to know," Leo said, tapping his chin.

"So, are we going to talk about it?" Leif asked, and I shook my head before I aimed. I wasn't good at mini golf, or regular golf. I didn't really understand using a metal—or plastic in this case—stick to hit a tiny ball towards a hole I couldn't see. But I had been outvoted, and the next time we had a guys' night, we'd be sitting down and doing nothing. Or maybe going on a hike. A hike could be good. We lived in fucking Colorado. There were mountains and trails everywhere.

"You're scowling. What are you thinking of?" Noah asked.

I glared at him, then swung, letting out a deep sigh as the ball hit the wooden side of the windmill and shot off into a bush.

"I would say you weren't really thinking of golf, were you?"

"When it's my turn to pick, we're going on a hike. Through the mountains, with backpacks and everything. Where we have to eat trail mix and be wary of bears."

Noah blinked at me. "If that's what you want. Lake doesn't like hiking, though. So I guess that's not something you'll do with her."

Tension rode my shoulders, and I let out a breath. "Really? That's where you're going with this?"

"Now I have questions, if we can bring it up. When did this start? How long's it been going on? Tell us more. Tell us everything."

I glared at Leif, who held up his hands.

"You're the one who kissed her in front of the windows at the shop. I didn't say a damn thing."

After lunch, when we walked back to the shop, I had indeed kissed her right there. I hadn't even thought about anyone else, so it was my own fault. Tomorrow night was her girls' night, and I knew she would probably be fending off the same questions. Only without a windmill and having to search for a ball in a bush.

I scowled and bent down, cursing under my breath as I scratched my arm on some holly and pulled out the ball.

"Who puts pointy plants right next to a place where kids could lose their balls?"

"Kids don't usually hit it that far off center," Leo said wisely.

I flipped him off and Noah clucked his tongue.

"No, no, no. We don't do that. There are children around."

It was after seven o'clock, and I looked around the empty place. "People are either getting ready for school tomorrow, or at home doing anything else."

"They should serve beer here. Beer would be nice," Noah put in.

"You're not even twenty yet kid," Leo growled.

"I will be in a couple of months. Finally."

I shook my head, set the ball back where it started, and hit again, this time without even bothering to look. It gently rolled down the drain through the giant hole, and the sound of the ball falling into the plastic cup echoed in my ears like a sweet relief.

"You just had to do that one-handed without looking, showoff," Leif teased.

"I hate you all."

"Seriously though, Lake does not like hiking. She likes sports, but she doesn't like hiking through the bush where anything could come and eat her. Not her thing."

I glared at Noah. "I know that. I've known Lake for a damn long time. I know what she likes and dislikes."

"Oooh," Leo said under his breath, and I moved forward, Leif holding me back.

"Okay. That's enough of that."

"Enough of what? You all teasing me?"

"We're not teasing you. We're just genuinely interested." Noah stared at me.

"I thought you guys didn't like each other. In fact, whenever the four of you came up with that scheme to start the business, I thought you were insane. I mean, you and Leif made sense, even Sebastian made sense, and I understood Lake wanting to be part of it because she's brilliant and understands business, but her and you? I didn't see it."

"Then you are blind," Noah laughed.

I looked over at my friend. "What?"

"You guys fought because of the sexual tension."

I stared at him blankly.

"That couldn't be further from the truth."

Leif whistled through his teeth. "I don't know. I mean, I'm not exactly surprised the two of you are finally doing whatever it is you're doing. And no, I do not want details."

"I want details," Leo said quickly before he held up his hands. "But not creepy details. Respectful details. And it's not because I'm afraid of you. I'm actually quite afraid of Lake."

I stared at the lot of them and just shook my head.

"You guys are insane. I really don't want to talk about this."

"Then don't. I think it's kind of cool," Noah said,

and I stared at him.

Leif cleared his throat. "The two of you are two of the most important people in my life. I love you both. And I trust you both. And it's none of my business."

I stared at him. "You're being very careful with your word choices right now."

Leif snorted. "So damn careful. It's not my business. It doesn't need to be my business. You don't need me in your head when you're doing this. Like when I first started dating Brooke, you didn't get into my head. You were there if I needed you, so I'm going to do the same with you. I will just happen to do the same with Lake, and it's weird. I'm not in the middle. If I was in the middle then I'd be placing myself there and it'd be on my own shoulders."

"You're talking in circles now," I said through gritted teeth.

"Maybe. But I love you both. So I guess I'm happy for you both."

He nodded as he said it, as if that was the end of the conversation, and frankly, it was as much an end as I wanted.

"Okay, since Nick finally finished this hole, it's time for the pirate ship."

Leo shook his head. "No, the waterfall is next."

Noah snapped his fingers. "You're right. We shouldn't miss the waterfall."

I looked at Leif, wide eyes. "There's a waterfall? How long is this?"

"We paid for the full eighteen holes, bud. Better get used to it."

I rubbed my hands over my face, barely holding in a scream. "Why isn't there beer?"

"Because it's a family-friendly and dry establishment."

"Next time one of your family members forces me to come here, I'm bringing a flask."

Leif snorted. "We'll bring two flasks."

Noah called out. "I heard that. This is a rocking-good time. Let's have fun."

I mouthed the phrase *rocking-good time*, and Leif threw his head back and laughed as we headed to the next hole.

I was not a miniature golfer. Not even in the slightest. I lost by a staggering amount and knew I was going to continue to lose until the end of my days.

And since I lost, I got to pay for dinner, even though I hadn't agreed to that. But I didn't care. Not when I knew we would take turns.

We ended up at a sports bar, with baseball of all things, on behind us. None of us cared about the game, but we watched a little bit anyway and gorged ourselves on wings, while I dug into a salad.

Noah looked at me, confused. "Why are you eating

that green and leafy thing at a sports bar? You've only had a couple of wings."

I swallowed my ranch-covered lettuce and followed it with a sip of beer.

"I'm in my thirties now. I'm trying to take care of myself."

"As soon as you hit thirty, your body starts to fall apart?" Noah asked, and Leif reached around and smacked the back of his cousin's head.

"When you're twenty-five, you hit a new low. Your body starts to break down. Then thirty, then thirty-five."

I nodded. "In other words, every few years, your body breaks down just a little bit more."

"Yes, soon you're going to know when rain is coming because of your joints," Leo added, and I snorted.

"And I wanted a salad. Mostly because I get heartburn if I just eat french fries and wings. And I don't really like fries."

The three guys stared at me.

"What?"

"How did I not know about this?" Leif asked, aghast.

"I'll eat french fries if they're there, but they're not my favorite thing. I like steak fries, and sometimes I'll eat freshly cut fries cooked in peanut oil. But they have to be really good for me to want them. If I had a choice, I'd pick onion rings, but they don't have the beer-battered onion rings here anymore, so I went with the salad. Yes, I've hit a new phase of my life—get over it."

"So I guess gone is the era of rare steaks, a cigar, and a bourbon?" Noah asked as he drank his chocolate milk.

"First off, you're drinking chocolate milk right now."

"It's actual chocolate milk. Milk where they add chocolate to it. I'm going to drink this. It's damn good."

"And you don't have a dairy allergy, at least yet," Leif put in.

Noah's eyes widened. "Wait. I could have a dairy allergy?"

I nodded. "A lot of times you can grow into a dairy allergy or a lactose issue. You do realize that half of your family, even with their cheese boards, pop a pill so they can enjoy cheese to the fullest."

Noah looked between us. "Am I getting older?"

"Oh shut up," I growled. "I'm not even old. It's just we're actually taking care of ourselves. And bourbon and a rare steak sounds fucking amazing. Not so much the cigar."

Leif grinned at me. "Probably because we stole one

from our friend's older brother, and smoked it in my backyard when we were 'camping,' and threw up because it tasted like socks."

Leo and Noah both laughed as I shuddered.

"It was horrible. The worst thing I've ever had."

"What did your dad do?" Noah asked.

Leif winced. "I was grounded. But he and mom both agreed that Nick and I were practically green, along with our friend Jordan."

I nearly gagged, thinking about it, and took a sip of my beer. "Seriously, everything that we'd eaten for dinner, and all the junk food, came right back up. Haven't had a cigar since, and I don't plan on it."

"So I guess no cigars when Sebastian's baby is born?" Leo asked.

I laughed outright. "First off, I'm so glad that is out of style. Second, I'm pretty sure Marley's parents would disown the Montgomerys even more than they're already trying to."

I gave Leif a look, who just rolled his eyes.

"Sebastian's been telling me some about it, and I hate that for him. But no matter what, Marley's parents are just going to have to get used to the Montgomerys. We're a force."

I nodded and finished my salad. "Pretty much. Don't worry. That kid is going to be taken care of no matter what."

"Okay, so let me get this straight, when I hit thirty, I'm going to have to actually start taking care of myself. I'll take note. And you and Lake are dating, but you're not going to talk about it. Fine, anything else I missed?" Noah asked, and I flipped him off.

"You are just a ray of information and sunshine, aren't you?"

"Maybe. But I like that you're the center of attention instead of me right now."

Leif leaned forward. "Is there a reason you should be the center of attention?" he asked.

Noah stiffened before he shook his head. "Me? Not at all. Everything's fine."

I looked at Leif, who shrugged. Everything wasn't fine with Noah, but he wasn't about to share. And I wasn't going to bug him about it because, frankly, that meant that Noah would find an opening to find out more about me.

And I didn't want to talk about it.

I didn't want to talk about Lake, didn't want to talk about my mom, didn't want to talk about anything like that.

When we finished eating and I paid, despite the fact that all three of them tried to pay for their meals anyway, I headed back home feeling weird.

I was usually the one in the background, the one that people didn't really notice. I didn't like the fact that people were up in my business now. Wanting to know more about me and caring what I was doing. It was weird.

When I got home, I quickly showered, tired from the day, and got into bed, wondering if this was going to be my life now. An odd night with the boys when I could, work, and being home alone.

I frowned, knowing that wouldn't always be the case. I could text someone. And maybe I would. Even if I didn't know what the fuck I was doing.

I pulled out my phone and sucked in a breath.

Me: *You up?*

Lake: *Is this a booty call?*

I laughed outright, my whole body shaking.

Me: *If you want it to be.*

I could practically hear her laughter as she texted back.

Lake: *I have had the longest day, I had to be up for a meeting on European time zones. I wish this was a booty call. Maybe I could release some of this tension.*

I quickly called her, not in the mood to text with my giant thumbs.

"Okay. Do you want to talk about your day? Or more about your booty call?"

Her laugh did something to me. What? I didn't know, and it should worry me.

"How was the night with the boys? Did you go to a strip club or something?"

"First off, I'm never going to go to a strip club. Not my thing. So you don't have to worry about that."

She let out a breath. "You know I really wasn't worried. That doesn't seem like your thing at all."

"It's not. No, we went miniature golfing."

She was silent for so long that I wasn't surprised when she broke out into laughter.

"Shut it."

"Did you at least win?"

I was silent for so long that she continued to laugh.

"I didn't. I failed. Whatever."

"It's okay. I'm decent at miniature golf. I can show you the ropes."

That made me smile. "You know, Noah was telling me how he uses it to pick up women. So he can wrap his arms around her and show her how. Guess you're going to have to wrap your arms around me."

Who the hell was this guy flirting? This was not me, but I didn't mind it. It was new. Different. And fuck, this was Lake.

"I can try that. I'm sorry that I haven't really seen you this week. It's been a little busy, getting the café up and running. And just all those meetings after the event."

We had only been on a couple of dates since we had gotten back, and I had only kissed her a few times. We hadn't done more beyond kissing. But I knew this was our life. We were busy, so we were getting used to it.

"It's okay, Lake. You don't have to apologize for being a high-powered kick-ass boss."

She laughed like I wanted her to. "That's nice to hear before bed. I really wish I was there. Which is not something I would normally say over the phone. But for some reason whenever I talk to you, I get all this courage."

I smiled. "Oh yeah? What would you do if you were with me right now?"

She sucked in a breath, and without thinking, I slid my hand over my boxer briefs, squeezing my dick.

"I've never actually talked dirty on the phone before. I don't know what to say."

I hummed. Low, deep. "I haven't either, but I'm sure we can figure it out. Should I ask you what you're wearing?"

Her laugh was soft. "A tank top and panties. The tank top's old, it has a few holes in the bottom, and my hair's piled on the top of my head. So sexy."

I groaned, slowly slid myself out of my boxer briefs.

"Tell me more."

"Are you touching yourself?" she breathed.

"Yes, I am. I'm already hard thinking of you, and I have to squeeze the base of my shaft, so I don't come right on my stomach."

I heard her swallow hard, then a shift of fabric.

"What are you doing?" I asked, my voice barely above a breath.

"I pulled down my tank top and I have my breast in my hand, playing with my nipple."

"Am I on speaker phone?" I asked.

"You have to be. Because I'm sliding my other hand down my stomach, and I'm playing with the edge of my panties."

I licked my lips, stroked myself some more. "Slide your hand underneath the hem of those panties and feel those swollen folds. Tell me if you're wet."

"I already know I'm wet," she panted.

"Tell me anyway."

She did as she was told, and I groaned as she let out a small little moan.

"I'm soaked just thinking of you."

"Stroke yourself. Gently at first, imagine it's my fingers, just a brush of the tip of my forefinger along your clit, and then lower down your seam, before I slowly, oh so slowly, insert my finger inside you."

"Nick," she breathed.

"That's my girl. Keep going."

Her breathing came in pants at the end of the line

where I knew she was doing as I told her. My strokes got faster as we panted together, telling each other to keep going, and then she let out a little cry, and she was coming, and I smiled, squeezed my cock again, and pumped myself, coming on my stomach, hard, fast, and sweaty.

I lay there, trying to catch my breath.

"I'm sad I didn't get to see you come. Your nipples go this beautiful shade of pink when you do."

"Really?" she asked, as out of breath as I was.

"Really. And next time, I'm going to have those nipples in my mouth as I fuck you hard. And you're going to clamp around my cock, squeezing me until there's nothing left, and I'm going to hold you close and kiss and bite every single inch of you."

"I don't know if I'm ready for bed or all riled up."

I grinned. "I think I need to take a shower," I growled.

She let out another laugh. "That sounds good to me. Goodnight, Nick. I'll see you tomorrow?"

I swallowed hard. "Yeah, Lake. I'll see you tomorrow."

It took a second for her to hang up, and then I was staring at a blank phone. At the stickiness on my stomach.

I knew I was in trouble.

So much fucking trouble.

Chapter 13

Lake

"I'M SO EXCITED ABOUT THIS," DIANA SAID, AND I smiled through the phone on our video chat.

"I'm excited about it too. Big things are coming, and we are only a few short weeks away."

"At this point, I feel like there isn't enough time."

I nodded, excited, as I went through the spreadsheet. My team would be working on the final touches with Diana. She knew what she was doing, and I was just an investor. But Diana and I had started a friendship, and I enjoyed hearing more about the café and everything coming with it.

"You're coming to the opening day, aren't you?" she asked.

"Of course I am. You wouldn't see me anywhere else."

"And I take it you're bringing that beautiful man I saw walking with you that day?"

I blushed, my lips twitching. "That man you saw was just my friend." Diana gave me a look. "At the time...well...it's a long story."

Diana nodded solemnly. "I understand completely. I'm just being nosy."

I laughed, shaking my head. "I don't know if it's nosy, or just interested like everyone else seems to be around here."

"I hope you bring him. Mostly because I want to see his take."

"I don't know if he's too much into fantasy or things like that, but I already told him a little bit about what it's about, so he'll be excited."

"That's all that matters. Even if it's not your thing, we want you to be interested enough that you'll come for the good food and the sometimes subtle, sometimes not-so-subtle ambiance."

I snorted. "I think you've found the perfect middle ground."

"I think I did too. Now, to go through a few more

things, and I'll leave you be. I know you've had a long day."

I nodded and absently rubbed the back of my neck.

"I had a few early meetings, but nothing I can't handle."

"If you're sure."

"I'm sure. Let's go through these, and then you'll be working with my team for the rest. And I'll see you on opening day."

"Perfect."

She clapped her hands excitedly, and we went through the last parts.

Diana and I finished our meeting quickly soon after, and I did a few things on my list, knowing that the next day I wanted to head to the shop.

I penciled it in and chuckled because I would see Nick later that night. I had dinner with the girls at my place, and Nick had a late evening tattoo scheduled. And after, he would come over and we'd have a drink. I didn't know what would happen then, only that I blushed thinking about it. I knew what we had done the night before when I was alone in my bed. The first time I'd ever had phone sex, it was with Nick.

But before anything else could happen, I had dinner with the girls.

I packed up my things, said goodbye to my staff, and headed home. Most nights, I worked far later than this, but tonight was girl time. And then Nick time. Somehow I was going to find a way to balance all three, even if I might fail just a little bit. No, I wouldn't fail. I *didn't* fail. I couldn't. Not when things were important.

I made it home, promptly put my things away, and began cooking dinner. I had a quick recipe for French onion soup, would pair it with a spring salad, and finish it off with the crusty bread that Brooke had promised to bring with her.

I chopped and minced and worked on my soup, thankful that this one didn't take forever. The secret was Worcestershire sauce. I had turned on an audiobook and listened to my heart's content, feeling relaxed for the first time in a long time.

Tonight was about friendship, girl time, and then later, maybe something more.

The doorbell rang, and I wiped my hands and looked at the screen.

Brooke stood there, May at her side.

I quickly ran to the front door, opened it, and grinned.

"You're here!"

"And we have bread. All the bread," May said.

May might be Brooke's nanny, but she was also our

friend. I liked the dynamic that we had, and I truly enjoyed being with these women.

They walked in, we hugged, and soon wine was flowing, and my other two guests, my cousins Daisy and Aria, came as well. Aria was Sebastian's twin. I had more than a few cousins and tried my best to hang out with all of them. I might only have two of them over tonight, but I knew I would see the others soon. We were spread out over most of Colorado, with some of us even out of state for college, but in the end, Colorado was our home, and we usually ended up back here.

"Okay, tell us about Nick," Brooke said quickly, breaking the ice.

I laughed outright and sipped my pinot noir. "I don't think I will."

"Are you quoting Captain America's Chris Evans again?" Daisy said as she leaned forward.

Daisy, like me, came into the Montgomery family later in our childhood. But it didn't matter because we were Montgomerys through and through, addicted to cheese and being in each other's business.

"I might be quoting Chris Evans. I can't help it. He's just so dreamy."

"But not as dreamy as Nick," Brooke said pointedly, taking a sip of her wine.

"You guys are terrible."

"No, we're not. We're nosy. There is a difference," May said with a laugh.

"Fine. You guys are ridiculous."

"Maybe, but tell us." Daisy leaned forward, her eyes intent.

"There's not much to tell. We're not putting a label on it."

All four women groaned.

"What is that?" I stared at them, narrowing my eyes.

"Was it his idea, or yours?" Brooke raised a brow.

I frowned. "Maybe his. But mine too. You know how stressful it is to date these days?"

May laughed. "I'm a serial first-dater, so yes, I do."

"At least you didn't get a second date with Leif. That's all that matters," Brooke said as she winked.

I winced. "I still feel like I should apologize for setting you guys up on that blind date."

"No, no, it's fine. I like being able to hold it over Leif's head. It gives me joy," May said with a laugh.

I shook my head. "You guys are ridiculous. And we're not doing labels. We're seeing each other."

"Exclusively?" Daisy asked.

I froze. "I don't know. I think so."

Alarm shuddered through me, but Brooke shook her head.

"Even if it's not explicitly exclusive, Nick doesn't

play that way. He never goes out with more than one woman at a time. I can promise you that."

I stared at Brooke. "How do you know that?"

"Because Leif and I talked about it. And you know that—you've known Nick longer than me. Longer than any of us."

"You're right. I'm just making myself nervous for no reason."

"You're at the beginning of a new relationship, even if there are no labels," Daisy added on quickly. "Your mind is going in a thousand different directions."

"I'm just trying to figure things out. Even if I feel like I'm losing my mind."

"Don't worry about it. You're allowed to be stressed out. It is kind of cool, though. Nick is hot," Daisy said.

"He is," Aria added.

I frowned at both of them. "Should I be aware of something?" I asked with a laugh.

"Just that we like your taste. Don't worry. He's a little too old for us."

The two girls looked at each other, giggling, and I scowled.

"Why did you just make me feel ancient?"

"We didn't mean to, but it is the truth. He's just a

little too old for us. But that's fine. We'll find our perfect men eventually."

I shook my head. "Hopefully, a long way away. You are still in college, Aria. You too, Daisy."

"Hey, my twin brother is practically married any day now, and I'm about to be an auntie. I don't think that time works the way you think it does."

"That's the truth," I said with a sigh as I sipped my wine.

"I'm sorry that Marley couldn't be here," I added as I looked over at Brooke.

She winced. "Me too. But tonight is her personal family night or something."

"They're probably playing Yahtzee and telling Marley once again that she's made a terrible mistake by dating that Montgomery boy," Daisy added, scowling.

I sighed.

"I'm trying not to hate them because it is sort of a little scary. One minute their baby girl is in high school and living under their roof, the next minute, she's in college and an adult and making her own choices. And oops, she's pregnant, but that boy loves her, so what happens next?"

"They're nineteen, or at least Sebastian is. Marley will be nineteen soon. It is young, it was unplanned, but they're figuring it out. Marley's parents were always like this," Aria growled. "And it has nothing to do with my brother. They want Marley to be in a box that Marley won't fit into. So they do all they can to force her into situations that she hates, so no matter what, it looks like she's making mistakes."

"I just hope she knows that we're here for her."

"She will if she doesn't already. Now, let's eat some of this soup that smells so amazing," Brooke said, changing the subject, and I was grateful.

There was nothing we could do about Marley or her family. Because we weren't in that situation, we would just be there when they needed us.

And frankly, I wanted to eat. That way, we could get to the next phase of my night.

Nick.

And everything that entailed.

DINNER WAS DELICIOUS IF I DID SAY SO MYSELF, AND I ate way too much bread. By the time the girls and I cleaned up, and they headed out for the rest of their evening, I was a little tired but excited.

Nick would be over soon. And maybe finally we could spend some time together that wasn't just over the phone. I barely had enough time for my personal life, but Nick's schedule was ridiculous too. Montgomery Ink Legacy was doing fantastic these days. Their waiting list was ridiculous, and though they did take time off for themselves, they didn't have a lot of time. As one of the owners, I was grateful because that meant I had profit coming in, and I could help make decisions about updates and the business side, but that also meant that finding an overlap of free time between Nick and me wasn't easy.

I finished cleaning up the kitchen, doing one last check to make sure I didn't have a speck of flour somewhere. I was a little messy when I cooked, but I liked a clean kitchen.

I swept up, knowing that this was just me nervous because I was waiting on Nick, and went to put the broom back in the closet. Something fell in the back, and I groaned, knowing it was one of the attachments to my vacuum that I had never used. It was one with spikes and I had no idea what it was for. I was probably going to have to look that up so I could figure it out. I bent over to pick it up, and everything froze.

It wasn't the only thing that had fallen.

A mint green shirt, a button-up that I hated. But his mother had given it to him, so he wore it on special occasions. But I joked once that he reminded me of mint chocolate chip ice cream, my least favorite ice cream, and he yelled at me. Had called me something I didn't want to repeat, and why couldn't I breathe?

I fell back to the floor, the shirt in my hand.

When had I picked it up?

My chest tightened and I gasped for breath, shaking.

Why was it here? How had I missed it? I thought I had cleansed my entire house of him.

Zach couldn't be here. Was he here? I could feel his hands around my throat, as he squeezed, as he told me that I wasn't worth living. That I wasn't worth anything.

I tried to breathe, tried to do anything, but there was nothing.

Something banged behind me and I flinched, curling into myself, the shirt still in my hand.

"Lake!"

It was him. It was Zach. It had to be him. Why couldn't I breathe? What the hell is wrong with me?

And then someone was holding me and I was screaming, pushing.

"No. No, no, no, no, no, no, no."

"Baby. It's me. It's Nick."

"Nick?" I asked, his name a light through the fog and I tried to suck in breaths.

"It's me, baby. I'm here. You're fine. What's wrong? Tell me. Are you hurt? Did you hurt yourself?"

Sweat covered my body, and my tongue tasted metallic, bile rocketing up my throat.

"You're here. How did you get in?"

He just looked at me, cupping my face.

"Are you okay? What's wrong?"

"I just…I think I had a panic attack."

He cursed under his breath as I tried to stop hyperventilating, though it wasn't easy. He held me as we sat on the floor, and I tried to figure out how he got in.

"What, why are you here?"

"I'm here because we have a date, and I saw you on the floor, not breathing." He blushed and held me close. "I sort of broke through your back door. You didn't have the deadbolt on, and I don't have a key to your house. I'm sorry."

"No, I'm sorry," I said, embarrassment rolling over me. He'd broken into my house because he had seen me on the floor, helpless. How horrible was that?

Tears filled my eyes and he cursed, holding me closer.

"I'm glad your family is in the construction business. They can fix things because I've no idea how to do it."

I kept crying, the adrenaline wearing off as he rocked me in his lap.

I hadn't even realized I was curled into a ball until he kissed the top of my head.

"Is this too much? Do you need me to stop holding you?"

At First Meet - Special Edition

I shook my head, leaning into him. He smelled so good, and I just wanted to wrap his scent around me and never let it go.

"No, it's not too much. I'm going to call my therapist in the morning, but I'll be okay." I let out a breath, annoyed with myself. "I'm allowed to have a life. I don't need to go out and party every night, but I'm allowed to do this. Why am I freaking out over a stupid shirt?"

He cupped my face before he kissed me softly. "It's okay. Everything's okay. I've got you."

"You do, but now you're spending your evening comforting me instead of us doing something fun. I'm just going to be too much for you."

He cursed. "If I'm not too much for you, then you're not too much for me. Hello, parental drama much? If I can handle it, so can you."

I blinked up at him. "So you're not going to deny I'm a lot to handle?" I laughed. I was laughing. How could he make me do that so easily?

"I'm a fuck-ton to handle. I think we can do it together. Okay? Now just let me hold you for a minute or two longer because you kind of stressed me out. But that means I get to hold you longer."

I swallowed hard and leaned into him and thought maybe everything would be okay.

That's when I knew I was in trouble because this

had been a long time coming, even in the few brief moments that we'd had together since everything changed.

I was falling in love with Nick.

I didn't know how long we sat together, him holding me, me shaking, before my phone buzzed on the counter.

He sighed, then reached up and grabbed it for me.

"Just in case it's an emergency. I know you're running the world and all."

I smiled, feeling better. Now I was just cuddling with him, even if it was uncomfortable on the floor. But I didn't want to stop.

"It's Diana. I wonder why she's calling this late?"

"Answer it. I don't mind."

I nodded, kissed his jaw, and answered.

"Hi, Diana, is everything okay?"

"I'm sorry to call. But the authorities are here. Somebody sprayed blood all over the outside of our café. I figured you'd want to know."

I froze. Tonight might have started off wonderfully, but had gone downhill fast, and it sounded like it wasn't over.

Chapter 14

Lake

I PACED THE AISLE BETWEEN THE TATTOOING STATIONS, knowing that others were looking at me, but I was worried. Worried about many things, but mostly about Diana and her kids.

"She's okay. She wasn't there when it happened. They didn't catch the guy on camera, but they took everybody's reports, searched, and you got it cleaned up. Medical hazard and everything. They're going to figure it out."

I looked up at Nick as he cupped my face and pressed a gentle kiss to my lips.

"Who tosses blood, actual *human* blood?"

"Where did they get the blood? That's what freaks me out," Leo said as he shuddered.

"I'm just so sorry that it happened," Marley added as she sat down at Sebastian's station. She had her hand over her growing baby bump, frowning. "It just makes me so upset that somebody would do that to a place of business that hasn't even been opened yet. You guys have put so much work into that, and I know that it's a dream to own a place. And then somebody is just trying to ruin it."

Sebastian, who sat next to Marley with their laptops open and research papers out, scowled.

"Plus, vandalizing the windows with human blood at a future vampire café? Too on the nose. What do they object to? The occult? Vampires themselves? Or do they miss the old restaurant?"

I pulled away from Nick as I saw people give us looks, because we were still a new item to them. The fact that Nick had openly kissed me in front of his friends at our tattoo shop was startling.

Mostly because I was still trying to figure out exactly how to act around him in public.

"I don't think it has anything to do with vampires themselves," I said, frowning.

Nick gave me a look. "Are you saying vampires are real?"

I rolled my eyes. "I'm not saying that. I don't know what's real or what's not in the supernatural. That's not my job. My job is to help get this business running. This is a single mom who has worked two jobs her entire life. She's going to kick ass at this café, and outside forces are not going to stop it. But it does worry me that somebody seems to be out to stop this."

"Does she have any enemies? Anybody that wanted that space? Someone from her past?" Leif asked.

"We don't think so."

Nick scowled at me, and I froze.

"What?"

"Do you think it's him?" he asked, and I swallowed hard, the others stiffening near me.

Leif cursed under his breath. "He wouldn't lower himself to do that, would he?"

"Who are you talking about?" Marley asked.

"My ex. Zach. But come on, first, he's in New Hampshire right now with his family. And second, he wouldn't do that. Do you know how much work that would be? No. That isn't something on his radar."

Nick continued to look at me, before he shrugged and went back to his station.

"Okay. It's not him. But it *was* someone. So you don't go to that place alone. You get me?"

Somebody whistled under their breath, and I glared at Nick. "Are you serious right now?"

"Of course I'm serious. You could have gotten hurt if you were there."

"But I wasn't there. Remember where I was?"

"I do. And I don't like the fact that we don't know who did that. So you're going to stay away from it."

"And you're going to stop telling me what to do."

"You guys, enough." Leif stood between us, scowling. "I know you love fighting, and I don't want to know if it's foreplay or not, because ew, but we are on a schedule today."

"Yes, we are," Brooke said as she walked in, clapping her hands.

"Oh, is it wedding-planning season?" I asked with a laugh.

Leo rolled his eyes before he went back to flirting with Marley, while Sebastian just snorted. Tristan and Taryn were coming in later in the day for their clients, and it was going to be a busy and profitable day for the Montgomerys.

But today was my turn in the chair.

"So we can talk weddings while Nick gets down to business."

Leo burst out laughing while Leif's lips twitched.

I put my hands over my face and screamed.

Nick just gently put his hands on my waist and sat me down on the chair.

"It's okay, baby. I'll just get down to business."

Brooke laughed outright while I just shook my head. "I'll be over in Leif's station going through wedding planning stuff before his client gets here."

"Mine's just walked in," Leo said as he walked up to say hello to a man who had to be half a foot over six-five. He was broad-shouldered, all muscles, and I gave Brooke and Marley a look, and each of them fluttered their eyelashes before Sebastian and Leif scowled at them.

I looked up at Nick as he gestured towards the back of the seat.

"Lay back, think of England, and I'll get this done quickly."

"You're just waiting for them to make jokes, aren't you?" I teased.

"Maybe, but you want the infinity symbol and open heart on your wrist. We're getting it done."

"I can't believe you stole my tattoo from me," Leif called out.

Nick shrugged. "I'm doing it. Get over it."

I looked between them and winced. "Okay, I guess we take turns?"

The Montgomerys were very particular about family tattoos. My first tattoo was done by my Uncle Austin down in Denver. Then my Aunt Maya did the second. Leif the third, and he was going to do this one as well since he designed it with me, but Nick had taken one look at the sketch, tossed it, and added something to it. He had then claimed my skin as his, not in a creepy way, and here I was, getting my first tattoo from Nick.

I was oddly nervous, even though I shouldn't be. He was one of the most talented artists I knew, gentle with his clients, and freaking brilliant. It was just odd to think the man that I was sleeping with, the man that I was falling in love with, was about to etch ink into my skin that would be forever. A permanent declaration of his craft.

I hadn't even told him I loved him. Not that I would for a while. No, I needed to come to terms with it first, and then maybe I could come to terms with everything else that came with being in love with Nick Gatlin.

"We'll be taking turns. I'm only letting you have this because..." Leif glanced over at his fiancé as Brooke glared at me.

"I do what I can," Brooke said as she pulled up the wedding notebook.

They just looked so happy, and I was grateful that I was going to be part of their wedding, even if it felt like everything was moving at an intense pace. Then again, I'd been lost in my own mind when they'd started their relationship.

"Let's go through exactly how today's going to go," Nick growled out, and I looked at him.

"Why don't you sound excited?"

"I'm excited. But also worried that I'm going to hurt you. I don't want to hurt you."

He whispered the last part so no one could hear, and I held back tears, my throat tightening.

"You're going to make me cry. I want to make out with you, and we can't do that right now, okay?"

He smiled and kissed the top of my head.

"Do you do that with all of your clients?"

"Well, George likes it when I kiss him, but that's because he asked nicely."

George was in his late 70s, had been through four divorces, and was currently dating at least six women at the nursing home. He liked to come in and talk ink and show off his full sleeves and back pieces.

I knew Nick had done a few of them, though George didn't get any tattoos anymore. He was on blood thinning medication for his heart, but he would just sit here and reminisce while everyone got to show him our latest pieces.

I sat back as he worked on the stencil and helped me figure out the exact placement. I had been thinking about this tattoo for over a year now, and it was finally here.

He looked me right in the eyes, nodded once, and

then got to work.

It didn't hurt. It wasn't that he was overly gentle because it was me. It was that this was Nick. And I liked the feel of the tattoo at my wrist, even though it hurt like hell when I had done my back piece. My nerve endings were weird that way.

When we finished, he went over aftercare, put the clear bandage on top, then smiled at me.

"Well, there's your fifth one down. You ready for more?"

I laughed. "A little bit at a time. I have too many tattoo artists in the family. If I let you all take turns so quickly, I'm not going to end up with any skin left."

"That's easy. I'm the only one who gets to do tattoos on you now."

"Bossy."

"Right."

"Well, you guys are adorable," a familiar voice said, and I froze, turning quickly to see my mother walking through the doorway.

Arden Montgomery was gorgeous with her dark chestnut hair and wide-set eyes. While I knew I looked nothing like her, and it wouldn't make sense if I did, I always figured I had her smile. Maybe it was just the joy that she exuded.

I jumped from my seat and ran to my mother. We threw our arms around each other and laughed as

Brooke and Marley came over, and then the four of us were hugging, and the guys were sighing behind us.

"All the giggling? What's with the giggling?" Leo teased.

My mother, sweet and demure and adorable, flipped him off and winked.

"I'm a lady, damn it. If I want to giggle, I can."

And that was Arden Montgomery. Kick ass and amazing.

"I didn't know you were coming in," I said as I hugged my mom tightly. Brooke went back to work on her things, her phone ringing, while Marley went back to work with Sebastian.

"I was in the neighborhood for real, and I wanted to see you. Is this the new ink?" she asked as she looked down at my wrist. "Leif did an amazing job."

"Nick did it."

My mother's smile brightened as she looked up at Nick. He had come to stand behind me, large and awkward, his hands in his pockets.

When he cleared his throat and held out his hand for her to shake, my mom just grinned and hugged his side. He froze for an instant, his eyes wide, before he hugged her back.

"Hello, Mrs. Montgomery."

"Arden. You call me Arden. You now have many Montgomerys in your life, you don't go by last names."

She patted his chest with her hands and stepped back. "I'm glad that I caught you. I didn't know you were doing the work. It looks lovely, Nick. Must be serious if you're letting him tattoo you," my mom teased, and I winced.

"Mom."

"What? I have four brothers who constantly did things like this to me. It's only my right as your mother."

"I would think if you're used to being on the other side of it, you wouldn't want to do it."

Mom shook her head. "No, I think it's time for me to have fun." She looked between us and grinned at Nick. "Well, Nick, you know I love you as Leif's best friend and co-owner of my baby's business, so I'm glad that I got to see you." She turned to me before I could say anything. "Baby, you're coming to dinner. Bring Nick."

I froze. "Mom," I began, and she shook her head.

But it was Nick who spoke, and I froze as he put his hand around my waist. "No, it's fine. I can do this, right? I knew it was going to happen sooner or later."

My mom just winked. "If I can handle a Montgomery family dinner, he can."

Nick cleared his throat. "With all due respect, if Liam can handle a Brady dinner with your four brothers, I guess I can handle this."

My mom burst out laughing before she hugged Nick tightly, and I just shook my head, mortified.

"I need to go, but I'll see you soon for dinner. I love you." She kissed my cheek, then went up on her toes to kiss Nick's cheek, then did the same with every single person in the shop, including Leo's client, before she ran out.

"Well. Erm. Okay."

Nick just grinned. "Come on. It's lunchtime. And you need to feed me."

"All this talk of food, I guess I'm hungry. And really nervous."

"Dinner with the family, *dun, dun, dun,*" Sebastian teased, and everyone began to talk at once. I just shook my head and grabbed my purse, running out of there.

When I got into Nick's car, he smiled at me, and instead of heading toward a restaurant, we headed to his place.

"What are we doing?"

"Oh, I'm going to eat, but I'm not in the mood for food."

"Are you serious?" I sputtered.

"You owe me."

I blinked, then followed him into his house before he pressed my back to the door and kissed me hard on the mouth.

"I owe you?"

"Hell yeah. I have to go to dinner with your family. And your mom just showed up being the adorable, amazing woman she was, and I couldn't say no to her. You owe me."

"And what exactly do I owe you?"

"Let's go with lunch." He went to his knees, and I shuddered.

"Just like that? That's going to be your lunch?"

"Damn straight." He slid my shoes off, and I stepped down to the floor, the luxury laminate vinyl cool underneath the bare skin of my feet.

"You make it hard to breathe," I panted as he undid the button on my jeans and tugged. I wiggled as he pulled my jeans and panties over my ass, and then my lower half was bare before him.

"Damn it, you're making my mouth water."

His head went between my legs and he was licking at my pussy. Just like that, no tender touches, no warning, he was eating me out and I could barely breathe, could barely do anything.

I licked my lips, shaking, as he spread me and continued to lick.

He had his hands on my thighs, keeping me wide as he looked up, his mouth still on my cunt.

His beard scraped against the inner skin of my thighs, and I was ready to come right there on his face. So when he slid his hands around me, spreading me from behind and playing with me back there, I groaned and then did come right on his face.

I shook, my knees going weak, and then I slid to the ground, Nick keeping me close as he held me. Then his lips were on mine and I could taste myself on him, shuddering in his hold. He pushed up my shirt, taking my bra with it.

"You taste so fucking sweet."

"I can't believe I came like that, so quickly."

"Let's see if I can do it again." He sucked on my nipple, twisting his tongue, making it hard to breathe. I shook beneath him, tossing off my shirt as quickly as possible. The fact that I was completely naked on his floor over his entry rug while he was still fully dressed should have concerned me. Instead, it just made me hotter for him and I could barely keep up.

"Damn it, you make everything just so hard to focus."

I smiled up at him, slid my hands between us as I cupped him over his jeans. "Speaking of hard."

He grinned before I squeezed and he groaned. I moved my hand, tugged on his shirt, and he knelt before my naked body, tossed off his shirt completely, and undid his belt.

"Don't forget the shoes. You're not going to be able to take off your jeans with them on."

And then we were laughing, pulling off his clothes

as we rolled on the ground, and I found myself strad-dling him. His cock was hard in my hands, as I pumped him once, twice.

"Are you going to ride me?"

"If you want me to."

He smiled. "I want everything, Lake. Everything." And then he slid his hands up my body, caressing my sides, my breasts, my neck.

It wasn't until I was writhing over his cock, ready to slide on top of him that I realized that his hand was around my neck. But it was gentle, and I knew this was Nick. He was testing the waters, making sure I knew that this was him. That he wasn't doing it for control, but to desensitize me.

A single tear slid down my cheek and he frowned, but I shook my head.

"I just, I need you."

He nodded and moved forward. "You have me."

"I need a condom." I angled to the side, grabbed my purse, and pulled a condom out. I had taken to carrying them with me because Nick and I weren't exactly the most scheduled when it came to being with one another. Sometimes life surprised you, and I wanted to be prepared.

I undid the foil with my teeth, loving the way that he laughed at the sight, and then I slid the condom over his length. I hovered over him, sliding my wet folds along his condom-covered cock, and we both shuddered. And then I was sliding down him, his cock stretching me, my body warm and aching. And when I was fully seated, both of us shook, and then I moved, riding him as I rocked my hips, moving slowly. I hovered over him, kissing him, letting him play with my breasts. He moved his hands back, spread my cheeks, and pounded up into me. Somehow we were both shaking, moving, and it wasn't pretty, it wasn't glorious, but it was perfect.

When I came, tightening around his cock, he followed, kissing me hard and holding me close.

I didn't realize I was crying again until he started wiping my tears away, and I knew I needed to stop doing that.

Stop crying when it came to sex with Nick. But it was hard when every time that we made love, I knew life was changing.

He was changing. And so was I.

I was in love with one of my best friends. And now I needed to find the courage to tell him, because finding that strength to fall in the first place had taken everything out of me.

So I let him hold me, and contentment washed over me for the first time in far too long.

Chapter 15

Nick

I HAD MET PARENTS OF THE PERSON I WAS SEEING before. After all, I was in my thirties and I wasn't a monk. I'd been in relationships before—even decently serious ones. Nothing I thought would last forever, but I had nearly been in love. I'd even been happy. I'd met Mom and Dad and siblings, smiling along and tried to act as if I knew what I was doing.

Sometimes they went well. Most times, they were the beginning of the end. It never made sense to me why someone would bring me to meet their parents when we both knew they wouldn't like me. It wasn't as though I was an asshole, but even in this day and age where politicians and celebrities had just as much if not more ink than I did, a lot of times parents didn't want to see their baby with a "tattoo artist with no prospects."

Those were the words one mother used while I was still in the room.

She had mangled the line from *Pride and Prejudice* as if I was going to end up with that man who loved his benefactor just as much as he loved potatoes. At least, that's what I remembered from the movie. Like everybody else, I'd read the book in high school, but I liked the Keira Knightly movie decently well.

I hadn't told anyone else that, because we liked to make fun of each other for the littlest things. Because we knew we could handle it.

Parents didn't seem to like me. I didn't know why. Maybe because I didn't have the same parental experience they did, but I had the Montgomerys. The Denver Montgomerys, that was. I knew Austin and Sierra quite well, as well as some of Leif's aunts and uncles. So I knew them, and they treated me like I was one of their kids.

I did not know the Boulder Montgomerys very well. It wasn't as if it was a very far drive between the cities. One could go from each of the Montgomery families in the four major cities of Colorado within two hours. Until you got traffic on I-25, and it took a little bit longer. But either way, the family wasn't that spread out. Some moved away for school or life, but they always returned.

I knew that Lake's father had moved away for a while to pursue a modeling career before he returned and became a bestselling author, and that Lake's mother had been born and raised in the same part of Colorado her whole life.

And I also knew that all of Lake's aunts and uncles on her mother's side lived nearby.

It was a massive family of connections that I was just on the periphery of, yet today felt weird.

I was nervous, and I had no idea why.

Oh, wait, I did, and it was because of her. Damn it.

"What's wrong?" Lake asked as we pulled into the driveway. I drove since Lake had needed to work and answer emails on her phone. I didn't mind that she worked even longer hours than I did. She was taking over the world with her businesses, so she needed to work for it. I was always here to ensure she didn't work too much and hurt herself.

Figuring out exactly how to tell her that without her kicking my ass was a whole challenge.

"I'm just fine. Is it really okay to bring cheese to a Montgomery house? I mean, I assume you already have a lot of cheese."

She put her phone in her purse and rolled her eyes.

"First off, there's never enough cheese. Second, it's just a joke between our families. I found this delicious apricot goat cheese from a local vendor that I wanted to try out. But honestly, you do not need to like dairy products to fit in with this family. You know that."

"I might know that, but it's still weird. It's an obsession."

We got out of the car, and I grabbed the canvas bag from the backseat, holding out my arm to help Lake maneuver the driveway.

Her parents lived in a large two-story home near the back of an older development where each neighbor had around an acre of land, and theirs happened to be full of trees with a tiny pond in the back. The tiniest of ponds, according to Lake. She had grown up in a different house, but as she and her siblings had gotten older and her father had gotten a little more famous, they moved into this gated development. What that meant was that some of the Montgomery reunions were now held here. Considering the size of the family, that had to be daunting.

"Are you ready?" she asked, and I shrugged.

"As ready as I'm going to be."

"Well, that sounds fun," she said with a laugh, and as I leaned down to brush my lips on the top of her head, just because I could, the door opened.

Liam Montgomery, in all of his six-foot-something, broad-shouldered, and inked-up glory, stood there, glaring at us.

"What are you doing to my baby girl?" Liam asked with a snarl, and I pulled away, straightening up.

Lake rolled her eyes, took the bag from my hand, and shoved it at her father.

"Oh, stop it." She went to her tiptoes, kissed her dad on the cheek, and then grabbed my hand.

"Come on inside and let him growl and grumble out here. He's like a bear with a thorn in his paw right now."

"I am not. Treat me with respect. I'm your father."

"Sir," I said, my jaw tightening.

Liam looked at me before his lips twitched, and he held out his arms.

I rolled my eyes and hugged the man tightly, slapping him on the back.

"Did I scare you? Did it work? I've been practicing that look in the mirror," Liam said as he moved back.

I snorted. "I'll be honest, at first, I nearly wet my pants."

"Well, next time I'll make you shit your pants, and we'll call it good."

I snorted while Lake looked between us, her mouth agape.

"Really? You're just going full-on bodily fluids."

"What?" Lake's dad and I said simultaneously before we looked at each other and burst out laughing.

"Men. I swear to God."

"That's what happens when you date a man like your father," Arden Montgomery said as she walked in, kissed Lake's shocked face, and moved to me. She hugged me tightly.

"I wouldn't say that. You just creeped your daughter out."

"But it's my job."

"Hey, are we making fun of Lake? I'm in. I have so many questions for Nick," Jemma said as she ran in. She was sixteen and all legs. She had a short pixie cut thing going on, but the last time I saw her, she'd had an undercut too. Right now, the pixie cut was bright purple with silver streaks, and I just shook my head.

"How do you get your hair to keep that color? Wait, why am I even asking? You look good, pixie."

She beamed and hugged me tight. "Thank you. And I have to take cold showers, which sucks."

"But at least she doesn't hog all the water like she used to. She's in and out, no lollygagging," Lake's brother said as he walked in. Anton was fourteen, already taller than both girls, and getting wider in muscle too.

"I see the spring training camp for football's going well," I said as I fist-bumped the kid.

"Decently. I could still use a few more muscles, but Dad says I'm not allowed to overwork it."

"You're still a kid. I expect you to gorge on junk food and rot your teeth; thank you very much."

Lake looked at all of us before she laughed. "I was a little nervous before this, but look at you guys, acting as if you've known each other for years."

I looked at all of them and shrugged. "I *have* known you guys for years. Though I will say, I am nervous."

"Why would you be nervous? It's not like you're defiling our sister," Jemma said as she skipped away.

Anton led out a groan as Lake's father froze, and I looked for a good place to hide.

"Jemma Montgomery. You apologize right now," Arden snapped.

Jemma nearly tripped over her feet and turned. "Wow. Mom voice and everything."

Arden narrowed her eyes. "Do it."

"I'm sorry for telling the truth," she mumbled.

"Jemma," Liam warned.

But it was Lake who spoke up. "No, no, it's fine. I'll get her later. When she least expects it. I'll take that fake apology. Don't you worry. I'll repay you in kind later."

Jemma's eyes widened. "I'm sorry. I'm really, really, really, really sorry," she said quickly, and I just laughed as the two began to playfully bicker. Because I had a feeling Lake would get back at her sister in the best ways possible, and everybody was just enjoying themselves.

"So I see you brought cheese," Arden said as she pointed to the bag Lake had set down.

I nodded and handed it to her. "It's some fruit and goat cheese thing. I'm not sure."

"Did someone say goat cheese?" Jemma turned, her eyes wide. "For me?" she asked, her voice playful.

Lake shook her head. "Maybe not. Little sisters who make fun of big sisters should know better."

"Is that my punishment? No cheese?"

Lake grinned. "No, I'll let you have that. Your punishment will come when you least expect it."

Jemma winced, then took the bag from her mom. "I'll go set the table..."

"I like the fact that she's sucking up to you. She's afraid. I like them afraid," Arden said with a mischievous grin.

I snorted. "You guys are a lot to take in, and I'm used to Montgomerys."

"Each of us is different in our own ways, so you're not used to us yet," Arden corrected.

As I followed everybody else into the dining room, the conversation turned to work and to life. Everything felt so damn surreal. What the hell was I doing here? I liked these people, I was friends with them, but Lake and I? We were still really new. And yet, I was already here about to eat dinner with her family as if I had done this my entire life.

Liam handed me a beer and raised a brow. "So. What are your intentions with my baby girl?"

Lake cursed under her breath. "Dad!"

"No, I want the answer. It's not every day you bring a boy home. Oh wait, you've never done it."

Unsaid was the fact that she had never brought Zach, despite how serious they were. Her parents had met Zach at a public event, but he had never stepped through these doors. And part of me was happy for that, a little prideful. But I didn't preen like a peacock.

"Well, we're friends. I'm not with her for the money. The only reason I'm here at all is because we've been friends forever and you know me. And we're still new, so you can step off."

I hadn't meant to add that last part, even though I grinned as I said it.

Lake's eyes widened as her two siblings stood beside her, mouths open.

Arden looked between us as if we were entertainment, and I had no idea if she was going to slap me upside the head for mouthing off like that.

But instead of saying anything, Liam just burst out laughing.

"Okay then. I didn't ask, but you've got this."

Lake moved between us, her gaze befuddled. "Excuse me? You guys don't get to growl over me. He's not my owner. You're not getting a dowry. And oh my God, we're just dating."

I rolled my eyes. "You're amazing and I'm an asshole. Get over it."

Lake looked at me and sighed. "Really?"

Her father cleared his throat. "You're the one dating a tattoo artist, Lake. You know how our family is."

Lake cringed. "Oh, God."

I just laughed and knew that dinner might be better than I expected.

———————

LATER, FULL OF CHEESE AND OTHER DELICIOUS FOODS, I held hands with Lake as we made our way up to her place. We had spent the night at my place the night before, but Lake had an early morning meeting, so she needed to be closer. We were falling into a routine and it confused me, and yet, maybe it should have been this way long before this. Maybe I shouldn't have been such a coward and done something about it.

As we walked inside and set down our things, she turned to me.

"That went amazing. Way too amazing. And it seemed a lot more important than I thought it would be."

Understanding, I nodded. "Yeah. I guess it was a lot more of a thing than we planned on."

"It doesn't have to be a huge thing. We haven't changed, and I know that we keep saying we're still new, but we've been friends forever, Nick. I guess there are expectations from others. We don't need to put them on ourselves."

"Yeah. I get it." I leaned down and brushed my lips against hers.

There was a problem with that. A damn problem.

I was already falling in love with her, and there wasn't a damn thing I could—or wanted—to do about that.

But one day, she would wake up and realize exactly what we were doing. And she would figure out that the princess in the tower, with the great family, the thousands of connections, and the millions of dollars in the bank, wasn't going to want to stay with the tattoo artist next door. And that would be fine. Because we would always have to be friends. We owned a business together, and I was one of those connections.

But I wasn't sure what I would do when she walked away.

When there was nothing left.

Pushing those thoughts from my mind, I kissed her, picked her up, and carried her to the bedroom.

She smiled up at me, dreamy-eyed. "What are you doing?"

"What I should have done before."

I slowly set her down on the floor, her shoes long since fallen off, and kissed her softly, just needing to touch her.

Why did this feel like a goodbye? It didn't need to be. And yet, it felt like it should be. Because people put all those thoughts and expectations on us, and one day she would wake up and realize she could do better. She would leave, and she would need to. So I would take tonight. Because I had a feeling that the worry on her face was from when people kept talking about the future, kept talking about things like a dowry.

She didn't want forever. She thought she had wanted it with Zach and it hadn't worked out, so she wasn't letting herself want it with me. But I would let myself have tonight.

Before it all fell apart in the morning.

It didn't matter that tonight had gone well, I just

had this feeling that she would wake up and realize that I wasn't good enough for her.

She looked at me, confusion in her gaze, but I didn't want her to think about anything else. I kissed her again, this time a little harder, this time a little more needing. We stripped, her soft cotton dress falling to the floor. I licked at her nipples, sucking and biting.

"Nick?" she asked, her voice urgent, questioning.

"I just, let me need you."

I hadn't meant to say the words, and as she searched my face I was afraid she would see what I didn't want her to see. What I didn't know existed.

I stripped her out of her panties, took off my shirt, and toed off my pants. I stood there in my boxer briefs, and lifted her into my arms. She was so light, so tiny. So fucking breakable.

But I didn't want to think about that. I couldn't think about that.

I set her on her dresser so I could see the long lines of her back in the mirror. I freed myself from my boxer briefs and reached for the condom I had already pulled out, sliding it over my length.

"Nick, it's okay. I'm here."

I shook my head and met her gaze as I slowly entered her. She was a hot wet vise around me, clenching me. She was wet and wanting me. Just a few kisses, a few touches, and she was already needing me.

But it wouldn't last.

It never lasted.

I moved, meeting her thrust for thrust as we shook the dresser, the stack of towels she had set there earlier falling to the ground. I cursed under my breath, lifted her up, still balls deep inside her, and set her on the edge of the bed. She let out a little oof, but I kept going, needing her, not wanting to stop. She wrapped her legs around my back, crossing her ankles, and then she gripped the edge of the bed. I pounded into her, needing her. Her breasts bounced, her body shook, but all I wanted was for her to come. To watch her body blush and her nipples tighten as she orgasmed around me. I needed to fuck her, to claim her, but I wouldn't. Because she wasn't mine.

And that was the one thing I always had to remember. Because she was Lake, the princess, and I was just fucking me.

She came, clenching around me, hugging me tightly as she moved her arms around me. She slid her hands through my hair and kissed me, and I broke.

Right then and there I broke.

I was falling in love with my best friend. The one woman I knew I couldn't have.

The one woman who I fought with more than anything.

And the one woman I knew would leave me when she realized exactly what she wanted.

I wouldn't be that person.

It didn't matter that I had accidentally begun to fall for her when we first met. Because she would walk away, like she should. She would be whole, and I would be fractured.

Just like it was always meant to be.

Chapter 16

Lake

I WOKE UP WITH STRONG ARMS WRAPPED AROUND MY body, holding me close.

This was different than before. Different than any morning, and yet it felt like home. As if this was what we should have been doing our entire lives.

Or perhaps I was reading too much into it.

This couldn't be my life.

His arm tightened slightly and I sank into him, breathing softly as the light peeking between the blinds shone on my face and I yawned.

"Good morning."

I hummed softly at the feel of the vibrations of his chest against my back. There was just something so primal and sexy about that. That he was so close to me, holding me. This felt right.

And yet, it was still so new. Had we fallen into this in the weeks we had been together?

Or was this what it should have been this entire time?

I didn't have answers for myself. And perhaps I should have. And yet, it was hard for me to focus with his hard length pressed against my backside and my body held tightly by him.

His hand slid between my breasts, cupping me, before sliding right back down in between my thighs. I arched against him, groaning, and then our alarm went off.

This time we groaned for an entirely different reason before I turned and looked at him. "Hi."

"Good morning," he replied. He slid my hair from my face and something clutched in my heart. I wanted to say something. Anything. To tell him what I felt. Only, it was too early. I made that mistake before, with Zach, and while I would never compare the two situations or the two men because there was nothing to compare, I couldn't help it.

"I have a tattoo appointment at 8:00 a.m. because I'm an idiot."

My lips twitched and I ran my hands over his brow, his shoulders. I needed to stop touching him but I didn't want to.

"You have it at 8:00 a.m. because your client has appointments with their doctors and then time with their kids every afternoon and for the rest of the week. And many people start work at 8:00. I usually start even earlier than this."

"We did have a late night," he grumbled, kissing me softly.

"Just a little."

The night before had been spent wrapped in each other, tasting one another, and forgetting all of our worries and responsibilities. I knew we would have to actually deal with those worries and responsibilities decently soon.

If we didn't, it was going to be a problem.

"Okay, I guess I should get up and go get ready for the day."

He reached around and gripped my hip.

"It would probably be prudent."

I smiled. "Really. Prudent?"

He rolled his eyes. "Look at you, rubbing off on me with all your smart words."

"Why do you say it like that? Why do you think that I am smarter than you?" I sat up, the sheet falling down so my breasts were bare in front of him. But I wasn't really thinking about that, I was thinking about him. And the fact that I might have hurt him.

He shook his head. "Don't worry about it. I don't have coffee yet."

"That's not an answer. We both have the same degrees, you know."

"And we also both know that school has nothing to do with being smart or not."

"That's true. So I don't know why we're having a problem."

"I'm not having a problem. I'm just not awake yet. We're good, Lake. Breathe." He sat up, kissed my nipple, then my lips, and I rolled my eyes before he pulled away.

"I'm going to go use the guest shower if that's okay."

Cold, I stared at him. "Oh."

There was a world of hurt in that *oh*, and I hated myself for letting it slip.

He shook his head, grabbed his clothes, then kissed me again. "The reason I'm doing that is because we both have meetings this morning and if I go in that shower with you, I'm going to fuck you against the wall and then eat you out until you're coming all over my face and I'm going to need two showers to clean up. So rather than licking your pussy and fingering you until your knees go weak and you have to spend another hour getting ready, I'm going to go shower by myself."

I blinked, looked down at his very hard cock straining against his boxer briefs, and swallowed hard.

"Oh." And that was a new wealth of information in that *oh*.

"Yeah. Oh. Let me go stop thinking about you on your knees as I fuck your mouth. I have things to do, and I can't do that with a hard-on."

"That does sound like an issue."

He growled at me, sending shivers down my spine and right to my pussy, and then he left.

There was something seriously wrong with me, but I honestly didn't want to fix it.

I WAS ON MY SECOND CUP OF COFFEE, WHILE ALSO trying to stay hydrated because I knew with the amount of caffeine I needed this week, I would probably hurt myself.

My phone rang and I smiled at Susanna's name.

I answered quickly, leaning back in my chair.

"Susanna. I'm so glad that you called."

"Me too. We need to schedule a retreat where it's just the two of us, maybe our families. You can bring that big man of yours. One where we're out of the prying eyes of everyone that wants to cannibalize our companies, or think they're better than us."

"That sounds amazing. I should probably try to schedule that in, along with a few other trips with my friends and family that I've been wanting to take."

"There's never enough time, but as someone who's been doing this a couple of more years than you, make sure you make time."

I scoffed. "You're not that much older than me, you know that right?"

"I do know that, but with those years comes a wealth of responsibilities and experience. So my advice to you is take those moments. Work will always be there, and it will always seem like you can't put it to the side, but our lives can't be solely based around what we can do to achieve greatness. We also need to think about the rest of our lives and what that encompasses. So make sure you take those weekends. Enjoy time with your boyfriend, your family. And when and if you ever decide to have children, with your children as well. They're going to have more memories of you as a person that loves them than what you can give them financially. And now that I'm off my soapbox, let's talk about work."

My heart warmed and I smiled. "That's very good advice."

"I'm sure others have given you similar advice,

because I know your father, and he is always very kind to me."

"I didn't know that."

"I've only met him twice, and your mother once, and they were always the greatest. And I know that they take time for themselves and their children. So, you do the same. Now, let's talk about our next charity function. Because I have a few ideas for the school."

Elated, I pulled out my notes and we went through what financial things we would have to worry about, as well as the process of setting up the board of trustees and advisers.

It took a couple of hours, and I was exhausted by the end of it, but thrilled at the same time.

Afterward, I smiled into the phone as we discussed things that had nothing to do with work.

"So, I noticed earlier when I mentioned that big hunk of yours, Nick, you didn't contradict me. I wasn't sure the two of you were actually together last time, as it wasn't my business, and it still isn't, but I am being nosy now. How's it going?"

I blushed even though she couldn't see me. "Things are...well...good."

Susanna chuckled. "Oh my, all those pauses. Good is good. I'm glad to hear it."

"I know your husband has this whole career of his and does amazing things with it, but how do you balance both? How do you make sure that you are putting yourself first where you need to, but not forgetting others along the way?" I paused. "That sounds selfish when I say it."

"It's not selfish at all. We were just talking about you taking time for yourself and your family, but remember, I said yourself as well. You are your own boss, you have control. And you need to fight for it more than some others might. Finding the balance between who you are as a woman, a boss, an entrepreneur, a family member, and everything else isn't easy, but you'll find it. We each have our own paths that we've had to travel, and I know that yours hasn't been easy. None of us have had it easy, just some varying degrees of difficulty. But just know that we are here for you. Always. And I'm proud of you."

I smiled, trying to unravel the thoughts that kept binding together in my brain.

I was in love with Nick. I just didn't know if he loved me back, and if we would be good for each other in the end. Because all we did was fight when we weren't sleeping together, and while sometimes we could be sweet to one another, we butted heads more often than not. I didn't know if that was conducive to a future, but the scary part was that I didn't know if he wanted a future at all.

And that's what made me hold back. Because I had

been the one to start this, hadn't I? It was my trip that had started things. I had asked him for help more than once. Something I would prefer to have never done. So now I didn't know how to come back from that. How to change things.

I would have to ask. Only, that sounded like the worst thing to do ever.

I packed up my things for the day, and because I had a long meeting the next day I would work a little bit at home, before doing what Susanna said and actually relax. My phone rang and I frowned, recognizing Reynolds's number. He was the contact for my restraining order on Zach, and I stiffened, my body growing cold. I answered, telling myself I was just thinking the worst. That this wasn't the end of the world. That I could handle this.

"Ms. Montgomery?"

"Hello, Reynolds. What can I do to help you?"

"It's about your shop down here."

I froze. "Did somebody put more blood on it?"

"That and more. I'm sorry. The entire place looks destroyed. It's been severely vandalized."

My vision began to gray and I swallowed hard. "Did they figure out who it is?"

"My team's out now, and it looks like we might have video surveillance. I know you were putting some up, but this guy was smart, too fucking smart. Sorry for the language."

"Don't be. I'm coming down there."

"Thank you. We're going to have a few questions for you."

"Okay. Is Diana there?"

"She is. She needs you, which isn't something that I would normally say."

Reynolds was usually pretty stoic, which was what I liked. I didn't need a man to see me cry and tell me everything was okay. I needed a man to get things done, and he had gotten Zach away from me as much as possible.

"I'm on my way."

I hung up and made my way to the café, my hands shaking.

Who was doing this? Who would try to ruin this place? It didn't make any sense. As I pulled up and looked at the roped-off section of the street, I wanted to throw up.

He said it was bad, but I didn't realize it was *this* bad. Red paint or blood or whatever it was, was thrown all over the sidewalk and street and the building. They had broken windows, put bricks and boards all around it. They wrote words I didn't even want to say out loud, and all I could do was stand there and wonder who had so much hatred in their heart that they would do this.

I parked a ways away, and walked towards the roped-off section.

"Ma'am, this is a closed scene."

"This is my building, Reynolds asked me to come. I'm Lake Montgomery."

The man spoke into his radio, and nodded, lifting the tape so I could get through.

Diana was on the other side of the building, her eyes wide, and when she saw me, she ran to me, flinging her arms around my shoulders.

"Who's doing this? Who hates us so much?"

I held her back, and though my eyes were dry, my hands still shook.

"I don't know, Diana. But they're going to figure it out. We will figure it out."

"We can rebuild. Right? We're not going to let this stop us."

I saw the determination in the set of her jaw and I nodded tightly.

"Oh, we're not backing down. As soon as they let us, we're going to make this place shine."

"Ms. Montgomery," Reynold said as he came forward. "I'm going to need you to see this."

Bile filled my throat, as my hands trembled.

"Did you figure out who it is?" I asked, though I'd already knew. Some part of me had always known. He cleared his throat and held out a photo. It was grainy, most likely taken from the camera next door. I didn't want to touch it.

"Who is that?" Diana asked, leaning forward.

"His name is Zach. He's my ex-boyfriend. And you have him on camera doing this?"

Reynolds nodded. "He was slick last time, was able to use the shadows so no one could see, but this took a little more effort and he was spotted. Even in the late afternoon like this, with the way that your building is positioned, people walking by wouldn't have seen it until the very end. So yes, it seems to be him. We're going to take a few statements and look for him."

"I'm so sorry," I said, then I looked at Diana.

"This is all my fault. I'm so sorry."

Diana blinked and shook her head. "Your ex-boyfriend did this? The one who..." her voice trailed off, and then I remembered that we had spoken of what had happened to me in the past, because it had come up. We went to a similar support group, and so the subject had naturally come up into conversation.

So she knew of Zach, and I hated myself for it.

"I'm so sorry," I repeated.

"No. It's okay. We're going to figure this out. You know this man? Are you actually going to do something about it this time?" Diana asked Reynolds, her voice snapping.

"Diana," I whispered, and then I realized that no, this wasn't my fault. I was going to tell her to back down. Ice slid in my veins and I knew that ice would help me not panic. And that's what I needed to do.

"We're going to do our best. We're going to find him. He's not going to hurt you anymore."

I held back a scoff. "Find him. Make the law do what it needs to do to make sure he never does this again. I'll say whatever I need to, answer all your questions, but find him."

It took over an hour of questions which had answers I didn't have.

No, I didn't know where Zach was. No, I didn't know what he was doing.

No, I hadn't spoken to him since he tried to call months ago.

He wasn't in my life, and yet he kept doing this. He kept coming at me.

I just wanted this to be done.

When Reynolds walked away, and Diana took out her phone to talk to her children, I turned and saw a familiar scowling face at the end of the tape.

Reynolds waved him in, having spoken to him before, and I pressed my lips together as Nick walked forward.

"Why didn't you call me?" Nick asked.

"Those are the first words out of your mouth?" I

asked, my voice ice, devoid of emotion. There was something wrong with me, but I didn't want to name it.

"You could have gotten hurt, Lake."

"I wasn't here when it happened. I came here when the cops were already here. I'm safe. But this shop isn't, but they're going to find Zach and they're going to fix it."

"It's fucking Zach?" he asked, now yelling.

People were starting to stare and I raised my chin. "Stop it. This isn't on you."

"Then it isn't on you, either."

"Fine!" I let out a breath, my hands fisting at my sides. "I don't know why he's doing this, but they need to find him, and every time that I'm almost happy, he gets here and I just, I need a minute, okay, Nick?"

He looked at me then. "A minute. Are you kidding me right now?"

"I just need a minute to be okay."

"Okay, I'm going to stand right here."

"Nick…" I whispered, afraid. I didn't want him to see me break. I didn't want this to be on his shoulders. Because Nick put everything on his shoulders. His family, his friends, me. I didn't want to be a burden.

"I'm not going to let you be alone right now, Lake."

I turned to him. "I called my dad. He'll be here soon with one of my uncles. I won't be alone."

He looked at me then, his eyes so unreadable that I was afraid that I had broken everything. "Fine. But this isn't over. You know that, right?"

A single crack in my heart, breaking ever so slightly, my lungs tightening. "I know it's not. But Zach...Zach did this."

"And you didn't."

"I know. But I just need to breathe, Nick. This is all too fast and I'm scared."

He cupped my face and kissed me hard on the mouth.

"Breathe. Then we'll talk."

My father walked up and Nick began to walk away. I reached out, gripping his arm. "I'm not breaking up with you. You know that, right? I just need to focus."

He laughed without any humor. "I know. You need to be alone and think. I get that. It's what I do too. Then I'm going to fight anyway."

He left and I stared at my dad, wondering how the hell everything had changed from this morning, how everything had gone wrong.

And what the hell was I doing right now?

Chapter 17

Nick

"YOU'RE NOT EVEN GOING TO FIGHT FOR HER?" LEIF asked as he stared at me, standing over the small partition wall separating each of our shop's sections.

"There's nothing to fight," I said and immediately regretted the words as both Leo and Sebastian whirled towards me.

"Are you serious right now? Am I going to have to kick your ass for hurting my cousin?"

I winced at Sebastian's tone and shook my head.

"I meant we aren't fighting. I don't have to fight to get her back because she's not gone. She was overwhelmed and did what she always does when she's stressed out and turtled in. She literally climbed inside her shell and will deal with it later. I didn't want to get into it in the middle of an already volatile situation, so I walked away so she could breathe. It's Lake. I know how she acts. We've been friends forever. Yes, things have changed, but I walked away so she could breathe. Her dad was right fucking behind me. What was I supposed to do? Force her to listen to me and let me wrap her in cotton wool so that way nobody could fucking bother her? Because that wasn't going to work. No matter what I do, Zach is always going to be there. He's going to be stalking her memories because he hurt her. *He hurt her*, Leif. And we did nothing about it. We didn't even realize she was getting hurt or that the asshole was treating her like nothing. Did you know? No. None of us realized it. We just thought that something might be off with her, but we let it pass. All of us did. And that asshole is still out there because God forbid anything ever works in our favor. So no, I'm not going to fight for her because I have fought, and I haven't walked away. But I'm giving her the fucking space that she wants because Zach didn't listen to her, but I'm going to."

My chest heaved once I finished my tirade, and all three men just stared at me, mouths agape.

"That was so much information. I've never actually

heard you speak for so long at once before." Leo took a sip of his water and shook his head.

It was Leif, though, who looked at me, frowning. "I noticed that she was tired. That she looked sad. But when I asked her if she was okay, she lied. She lied because she was ashamed even though there was nothing for her to be ashamed about. So I didn't do anything. And that's on me. And I sure as hell don't fucking trust Zach or whatever connections he used to get out of trouble in the first place and is still hiding where nobody could find him. So I guess you did fight for her, just not in the way that we think you need to."

I sighed, ran my hands over my face. "I don't know how to be with her. She's Lake. I realize that she's your cousin, and not related to you, Leo, but still."

"No, we may joke around, but I think of Lake more as a sister than anything. You were the only one who thought different."

I sighed. "I don't know how to be with her. I didn't mean for this to happen. I just went on that stupid trip so she wouldn't be alone and no one would talk shit about her. Because God forbid she actually ask for help or lean on anybody until she's at the breaking point."

"Now it sounds like you're talking shit about my cousin," Sebastian muttered.

"But I'm not. All of you Montgomerys are like that. You wall yourself in to try not to lean on anyone else so you don't worry anyone. And yet you all need each other."

"It's like you're looking in a mirror, isn't it?" Leif said pointedly.

I snorted. "Maybe. Damn it. I don't know. I'm really not good at this."

"I'm not either, yet Brooke stays with me. Kind of lucky that way."

"Once the dust settles, and they find that man, and they let me beat the shit out of him before taking him away to jail," I began, and Leif grinned quickly before it faded into a scowl, "once all that happens, what's left?"

"You two are like, perfect for each other."

I looked at Sebastian, blinking. "Seriously?"

"Of course you are. You guys push at each other and bring out the best."

"I would say we've brought out the worst in each other," I grumbled.

"Not even. You guys challenge each other and are different enough that you'll never get bored. It was inevitable that you were going to date a Montgomery."

"I just don't like the fact that she could have been hurt."

"She wasn't even there, Nick," Leif said. "And she hasn't been alone since. You know her dad took her home, to the family home, and she's been hanging out with the cousins all day while working from there."

"And yet I'm not there."

"Well, that's something you need to work on. Why didn't she want to call you?"

"Thanks for making me feel like shit," I answered.

Leif shook his head. "No. Could it be she just went back to what was comfortable? Or that she was overwhelmed like she said. Just talk to her. Which I know sounds so strange considering I don't actually like to talk about my feelings and shit, but here we are. We're learning."

"It takes a village," Sebastian added, and I shook my head.

Thankfully the conversation was over, and Sebastian and Leif's clients both walked in, Tristan and Taryn behind them, their clients and Leo's following soon behind. My client was running late but would be there soon. I was grateful, because it gave me more time to think.

When the bell above the door rang, I looked up expecting to see my client, but instead I saw *her*.

Not Lake. Damn it. I wanted it to be Lake.

"Hey, we'll be right with you," Leo called out before his voice faded as he saw the look on my face.

"I've got this," I said while Leif gave me a look.

I shook my head and figured if I was going to force

Lake to deal with her own fears, maybe I should deal with my own.

"Mom."

"Hi. I didn't know if you were working today, but I just wanted to drop these off." She held out two canvas bags filled to the brim with photo albums. For some reason my heart lurched, and I wondered what was in those—and why part of me wanted to find out while the other part wanted to hide.

"There're a couple of boxes and stuff inside, just small stuff from your dad. They were in storage, but I thought you should have them. I honestly thought I would just drop them off with some of your coworkers here, and you wouldn't be here, so you wouldn't have to see me. Again, I'm sorry for encroaching on your space. But these are yours and you should have them."

I looked at her, at the woman she had become. She looked about a decade older than her years, but that was probably due to lack of sleep and the stress that came from breaking down after losing Dad.

But she looked nice, had done her hair, put on a little makeup, and had dressed herself in clean clothes. She looked like a mom. A memory of my mom. It was odd to see her here, especially when everything kept coming at me at once.

"Thank you. I'll take them."

Relief flooded her features until she schooled them again, and I hated myself for that.

"I just wanted to say I'm sorry again. I know I made mistakes. I ignored you."

I let out a hollow laugh, noticing that everyone else was doing their best to make noise as if they weren't paying attention, but they could all hear. I didn't want an audience for this, but frankly, I was done hiding. Done hiding from everything. From my past, from what I felt for Lake. Hiding wasn't doing any good, so maybe I should just be honest for one fucking minute.

"You don't really have to say anything. Thank you for these though."

"I was wrong, and I do not have any right to your forgiveness. But I wanted you to know that I was sorry. That nothing that happened was your fault, even though you know that. And I'm very glad that you had the Montgomerys." Her eyes filled with tears. She looked past me, towards Leif, and smiled. "I'm glad you had the Montgomerys," she repeated before she looked at me again.

"I lost myself, and then I lost you. And I'm sorry. I'll go now and you won't have to see me again, I promise. It's good to see you looking well. You're doing amazing things, Nick. Just like I always knew you would."

She turned to go, and I cursed under my breath. "Mom. I don't know…"

She turned to me then, that small sliver of hope in her eyes breaking me. "I know, Nick. It's okay. You don't have to say anything. This is on me, it was never on you."

"You know what, why don't we take a seat? My client isn't here yet, and I could do with some coffee." I paused. "You like tea, right? That rose tea?"

She stared at me a moment, her eyes wide before she smiled tentatively. "You have rose tea? I didn't think you liked that."

My chest hurt, but I nodded. "Lake likes it."

I turned and led my mother back to the break room, for a cup of tea, because why not? Hiding from the mistakes of the past wasn't helping. And I couldn't fix my past, but she was trying, and honestly, I didn't have anyone left. She was my only family. Yes, the Montgomerys were family, but she was my only blood. And she didn't have anyone else.

I couldn't fix what happened to Lake, couldn't fix what had happened to my dad, to my mom, to me. But I could fix this. And I would be there when Lake came back. When she realized that I would be there. Because I didn't want to go back.

I sat there with a cup of coffee, staring at my mom

as she sipped her tea, as the others worked, and I introduced them.

The door opened again and I turned, and once again it wasn't my client. It was Lake, and my heart hurt, everything hurt. But as she smiled at me, her eyes wide, I had hope.

Chapter 18

Lake

I STOOD IN THE FRONT OF THE SHOP, WONDERING WHY there were so many eyes on me and knowing that I just needed to get this over with. I should have been here earlier. I knew that. And Nick needed to know that as well.

I knew he was here, but I hadn't expected *everyone* to be here. So now there was no hiding.

"Hi, Nick," I whispered.

"Lake." Nick prowled toward me and my heart raced.

Sebastian moved out of the way and looked

between us, eyes wide. Leif stood there, an older woman next to him. Leo and his client, as well as Tristan and Taryn and their clients all sat in their sections, staring.

There wasn't even the whir of a tattoo in progress to drown out the screaming in my thoughts as I tried to think of what to say. I should have practiced this, but there wasn't any practice when it came to Nick.

"I just wanted to say I'm sorry," I whispered.

He scowled. "What for?"

"Oh fuck," Sebastian whispered before he let out a grunt. I assumed somebody elbowed him, though I didn't know who.

"What are you sorry for, Lake?"

"I'm sorry. I'm sorry that I pushed you away. I keep doing that, and I know you didn't fight right then because you promised you wouldn't. You promised you wouldn't control me like Zach did. But it's my fault that I walked away when things got tough. And I'm sorry."

Nick looked at me and put his finger over my lips. "Shush. Stop. Don't apologize."

I blinked at him. "I should have leaned on you. I should have called you."

"We both should have done a lot of things. Probably a lot earlier than just a few months ago." He let out a breath. "I love you, Lake. I might get growly and angry over things, but I'm not going to leave or feel like the world is ending because we get in a little fight. I'm pissed off that he did that, and if I could find him, I'd strangle him. Or maybe I'd rip out his guts, I don't know. But the cops better find him before I do. It doesn't matter. We'll figure it out, we'll help you rebuild. And I'm going to be by you no matter what. And I should have done something long before this. Long before you even fucking met Zach, but that's on me."

He continued to talk but all I could focus on was one thing. "You love me?" I blurted, feeling as though the floor were falling out from beneath me.

He scowled. "Of course I fucking love you!"

I blinked. "Well good. Because I love you too!" I was yelling at this point, and somebody snickered.

"Oh they're still fighting. Of course. At least we know some things will never change," Leif shouted.

"Fuck off, Leif," Nick called out then looked back to me. "I'm going to make you a promise. If I feel like I'm being an asshole, I'll try to step back, or you can tell me."

I snorted, I couldn't help it, even as my heart felt it was growing five sizes. "I do that anyway."

"That is true. However, just know that we're going to get on each other's nerves. We're going to make mistakes. But I'm done pretending. I'm done thinking that it would be better off if you were the princess in the tower and I was the farm boy."

"She ends up with the farm boy. I'm just saying,"

"She does, but I don't really look good in black leather pants."

"That I'm going to have to see," Leo called out.

I looked past Nick and grinned. "You know, I'm picturing a Halloween party at my house. Dress-up for couples."

I fluttered my eyelashes, and Nick scowled. "I love you. But that's a hard no."

"I'm hearing yes. As you wish?" I teased.

"Well, it's official, we've lost another one," Tristan said with a laugh.

Nick kissed me before I could think, and everything felt as if it was finally making sense.

I loved him. And he loved me too. How could I not have known?

"I'm sorry it took me forever to figure it out."

"Our trip wasn't that long ago," I corrected.

"You know as well as I do that this goes back far longer than that. I don't believe in love at first sight, but we had something at our first meet. So that should count for something."

"Hold on, I am writing that down," Leif joked. "Now that is a line. A truthful one, but poetry."

"Excuse me?" a soft voice said from behind Nick.

Nick stiffened, before he turned.

"I'm sorry to interrupt. I was trying to be good and not make myself known, but that was the sweetest thing I've ever heard, Nick."

I looked between them, as recognition dawned.

"You're Nick's mother."

She smiled.

"I am. And again, I'm sorry for interrupting. But I didn't know Nick could say something so sweet. You're right, Leif. I'm glad you're writing that down."

Nick cleared his throat. "Lake, this is my mother, Teresa."

I looked between them and smiled. "It's lovely to meet you."

I had a thousand questions, and from the pained look in Nick's eyes, he had some as well. But he would give me answers, eventually. It seemed like today was a day for many things and for many ways for our lives to change.

"So I guess this means that when we fight with each other, we don't have to hide it anymore?" I asked with a laugh.

"You were hiding it before?" Sebastian scoffed.

I laughed and leaned into Nick as his mother opened her mouth to say something, and glass shattered behind us.

Shards of glass slid into my skin, and I screamed as

Nick threw his body on top of his mother and me. I hit the ground hard, pulling his mother out of the way as more glass shattered.

People were shouting as another window broke, and then smoke began to fill the air.

"Oh my God, what is that?" Teresa asked as she sat up, blood pouring from an open wound on her forehead. I reached out and covered the wound, keeping her down.

"I don't know. Nick?"

"Fuck, get everyone out of here. There's a fire. Somebody threw a brick in the window, and I don't know...fuck, part of the side entrance is on fire." I coughed as I pulled Teresa up, and Nick dragged us out of the shop.

Debris fell as the fire licked up one side of the room, and some of the guys were trying to put out the flames though Leif and Nick pulled us all out. The whole place wasn't on fire, but enough of it was that if the authorities didn't get here soon, it was going to be bad. Little cuts covered my arms and side, and I looked up at Nick, my hands shaking as I reached out. He had tiny cuts down his body like me, and I let out a breath.

"I'm fine. Who the fuck did that?"

But I looked at him, and I knew.

"Are there blankets or something? Can we put the fire out?"

"You're not fucking going back in there," Nick ordered.

I counted everybody, my hands shaking as I coughed smoke out of my lungs. My adrenaline was beginning to fade. Nick's mother stood near us, the small box in her hands that carried their memories, but I couldn't think about that right then.

"Is everybody out?"

"We're all out. It's empty. But fuck, we can't put the fire out."

Someone running caught my attention, and I turned, and then Nick was running.

He didn't even look back, he just kept going, Leif right behind him, and I knew. I knew who they were following, who they had seen.

I looked at Nick's mother, at Sebastian. "Stay here and stay safe. Don't go back in there."

And then I followed after them.

"Don't you get hurt!" Sebastian ordered as he pulled Teresa to his side, keeping pressure on her forehead.

I was wearing heels, so running wasn't easy, but I kept moving, chasing after them.

And as I turned, I heard the shouting.

"Fuck you. If I can't have her, no one can!" Zach called out as he kept running, but Nick was faster, and bigger. He tackled Zach to the ground.

"Don't you fucking talk about her," Nick snarled. And then he punched Zach.

"I'll take you all. She doesn't deserve anything." Zach pushed up, smacking his head into Nick's chin. Nick rolled back, cursing, blood splattering, but Leif was there, pushing Zach back down, as Nick hit him once, twice, again and again.

"Stop it. Don't kill him!" I shouted as I finally caught up to them.

"He deserves it."

"Yes. He deserves a lot of things, but you don't deserve to go to jail. Come on, people are watching. The cops are on their way. We have to go see the shop. We have to save the shop. Zach's here, we have it all on camera. He's going to jail for a very long time." And if he didn't, I would find any other way possible to make sure he got there. Because I was done with this.

I looked down at Zach who glared up at me with bloodshot eyes.

"Fuck you."

"Scum, just like the rest of them," he spat, even though Leif had his knee on the man's throat. You're scum. You're nothing. You never deserved me. And you're going to rot wherever you go. You're just a bitch who wasn't even a good lay. I should have killed you when I had the chance, when your throat was beneath my hands, and I could have just squeezed a little bit more and then you wouldn't have breathed another word. You can have this low-life scum. My family will get me out of jail. It's what they do. Because you're nothing. You don't have my connections." As Leif pulled back to punch him, I kicked, my pointed shoe hitting Zach right in the balls. He let out a sharp gasp before he began to cry, and Nick looked at me.

"Okay then. You okay, baby?"

He looked at the blood on my arms, I looked at the blood and small bits of glass on his face.

"I'm okay. I promise you I'm okay. But let's never do that again." And I burst into tears. He held me as we waited for the cops to come, and I knew there would be a thousand questions to answer, countless things to go over, and I didn't know what we would do. But I had Nick, and that was all that mattered.

Because this was over, it was finally over.

I had first come to him when I had nothing in my heart, nothing in my soul. I had been broken, beaten down, and shattered. But Nick had been there, the one person I could ask for help. The one person I hadn't known I could.

And he had watched me grow into the woman I needed to be.

And he hadn't asked me to stop. Hadn't asked me to not be who I was. He had watched me make my mistakes, on my own, and had helped me stand up afterwards, by his side.

I loved him. I had loved him for far longer than I wanted to admit. Because Nick had always been there. The one man for me.

It had just taken me a long time to realize it.

And I was never going to take that for granted again.

I knew our future began right then, and our past didn't matter, because now was the only moment that did.

He was mine, finally.

Chapter 19

Nick

WE SAT AT LAKE'S HOUSE, HAVING A MONTGOMERY dinner of our own. Well, Montgomery and friends.

Everybody had pitched in with something, whether it be food, drinks, games, or helping make sure Luke, Brooke's son, was occupied.

It had been a long couple of weeks since the fire, and now decisions were being made, people were finally learning exactly what happened, and all I wanted to do was sleep. And wake up next to Lake. Which if I had my way about it would be every day to the end of my days. But she didn't know all of that yet.

She would, eventually. Once we found the time on our own terms. But we had started as a fake date, and would end up as the real deal.

Leo, Tristan, and Taryn sat outside near the fire pit, laughing at something. I didn't know exactly how things were going to work out for the shop, but I knew they would stay. They were family.

Leif came up to my side, Sebastian on my other.

"So. How's it going?" Sebastian asked, a little too nonchalantly.

I snorted, took a sip of my beer.

"Just thinking."

"I'm just glad that the fire damage wasn't as bad as we originally thought," Leif said after a minute.

I nodded as Lake slid up between me and Sebastian, and I wrapped my arm around her. She leaned against me, as our friends and family milled around before dinner was served.

"We can open up again soon after we add a few coats of paint and fix the windows. The water did the most damage, but with the floors that we chose, we're not going to have to redo them anytime soon," Leif said.

"That's true, though it's going to feel weird. A little different."

Lake sighed. "I won't say that I'm sorry because every time I do, you all yell at me."

"Damn straight," all three of us said at the same time, and Lake snorted.

"It's not my fault, and Zach's going to be in jail for a long damn time for many things, but the vampire café is opening soon, and our shop won't be far behind. And, I think I know what we can do next."

"Open up a new place?" Leif put in, and I froze.

I turned to him, eyes wide.

"What? You've got to be kidding me."

"I like our location, it's in a good place, but the building's getting a little too small for all of us, don't you think? When we got this place, it was the only place that worked at the time, but it was never perfect. The repairs on it won't take as long as we thought, not with the family in the business. I figure we will stay there for another few months until we find a new location. One where we can put in a café next door."

I looked between all of them. "Are we going into a franchise? Are we going to open up a café even though that's not in our wheelhouse?"

"I have a few feelers out there. Mostly the Montgomerys have a few feelers out there. But I don't know, I think this was a good place to start, and we'll work here for a few months once we open back up. And then we'll see what happens. But I don't know. I think we need a little bit more room."

I looked down at Lake, who smiled. "We can afford

it. Between the insurance payouts and our profit margins, I think it's time. This is a good starting point."

I let out a rough laugh. "Not in my wildest dreams would I have ever thought that we would've gotten here. But okay. We work at this shop for a little bit longer while we hunt for a better one. That's not going to be scary at all."

"I know that the family is working on a few other businesses, either extensions of what our parents have or what the cousins are thinking of building. So we'll look into it."

"Are we going to just make a Montgomeryville then?" I asked dryly as Lake burst out laughing.

"I kind of like that idea. Montgomeryville. It has a nice ring to it."

I shuddered. "Oh, please stop. I'm not a Montgomery. I know you guys tried to force me into it, but I'm not."

Noah came forward, his roommate Ford at his side. "Did we hear something about a town for Montgomerys?"

"Don't do it," grumbled Ford. "Once you're in, they never let you out."

I tilted my beer towards Ford. "Smart man."

Ford grinned and Noah rolled his eyes. "Well, we're looking for real estate as well, at least in the future. So let's talk."

I looked at him and frowned. "For what?"

"For reasons. Lake will help us. Not monetarily," Noah corrected as I scowled. She patted my chest at my overprotectiveness, and I let myself relish it. "But figuring things out. That's what she's good at. She's a genius."

Lake blushed and I laughed. "That is true. She's the smartest person I know. She has me, after all."

Everybody laughed, while Sebastian just shook his head. "You are very lucky that she's not going to yell at you in public."

"Do you not know me? I will totally yell at him in public," she added.

"Okay, that is true."

"Hey, Sebastian, baby? I'm exhausted. Do you think we could head home soon?" Marley came forward, waddling. "I'm sorry for interrupting. Pregnancy brain is a thing."

Sebastian hurried over, cupping his girlfriend's face. "What's wrong?"

"I'm just tired. And I know I'm hungry, and dinner's almost ready, but I think I just want to take a nap. I blame the baby. They keep pressing on my bladder."

Aria, Sebastian's twin, smiled and hugged the woman close. "It's okay. We'll take care of you. You can continue to make plans while I drive her home. Don't worry about it."

"No, I'll go with you."

Sebastian looked up at us and winced. "Sorry for leaving early. But the baby calls."

"I hope you're talking about the actual baby, not me. I hate being called baby," Marley said with a laugh before she turned to us. "Thank you so much for the invite. I think I just need to get better sleep. It's just hard to find a good way to angle the belly."

"You know those body pillows helped me," Brooke put in.

"I have the candy cane one, but I feel like I should have gotten the U-shape."

Lake looked between them, a small smile on her face. I leaned down and whispered, "Why are you smiling?"

"Just thinking. They are adorable, aren't they?"

"Are you thinking about what kind of pillow you want?" I growled.

She laughed. "Not really. Maybe. Let's get used to the whole being together and building up a new possible franchise, starting a school, opening up a café, and figuring out exactly whose bed we're sleeping in tonight. Then we can think about the future."

Everybody began to talk at once about their own lives, and I knew things were changing. That the plans

I thought we had made were probably out the door, and we were going on to bigger and better things. It was exhilarating and frightening, but I trusted Lake with everything. I leaned down and kissed her softly and she moaned into me. Somebody cheered, another person booed, but I just held Lake close.

"Well, we can always practice."

She giggled, somebody gagged, and I ignored them.

"You with the lines. I like them."

"I try. Now let's go eat, and then I guess we can figure out everything else. I'll do whatever you say. You just tell me where to put things. It's what I do best."

"Really? You're letting me make all the decisions? I love it."

"I must be in a haze. I didn't mean that," I teased, but she just laughed and pulled me into the dining room, where everybody started to pile food on their plates.

I smiled, laughing around with my family, and figured that this was okay. I might not have known where I began or how I had gotten here, but I wasn't leaving anytime soon.

I was going to marry that woman, I might not know when yet, and she might not even know it yet. But I would.

Although I wouldn't be a Montgomery, she could

keep the name, but I'd keep my own. For my mom and my dad. Even if I didn't get the name, I had the family.

That was the Montgomery way.

Even if it had taken me nearly too long to realize it.

Chapter 20

Sebastian

MARLEY GRIPPED MY HAND, AND I HELD BACK A WINCE. She was the one going through a contraction. I shouldn't show how much her grip hurt. But my word, the strength in her body—I didn't know how she was handling it.

"Oh, that was a bad one," Marley said as I reached for the cold cloth to wipe her face. Sweat covered her body, her hair in a frizzy bun on the top of her head, her skin alternating from a blotchy flush to a pale cream. The pregnancy had gone amazingly well. Other than the stress of everything, she did great. And here we were, in labor, about to be parents, and I still couldn't quite believe it. And I wouldn't change a thing. Because I loved Marley with everything that I had.

"You did great," I whispered before I kissed her brow. She was icy cold, even though her skin was flushed, and I frowned.

"You feeling okay?"

She gave me a look. "I'm about to push a cantaloupe from between my legs. I'm a little nervous, but I'm okay."

She sort of slurred the words, and I straightened.

I looked over at the nurse, who narrowed her gaze at Marley before she started saying things I couldn't understand.

"Marley? Marley. Sweetheart? What's wrong?"

Marley reached out for me, but she couldn't lift her hand, then her eyes rolled in the back of her head, and all the machines around her started beeping.

My stomach fell, and I swallowed hard, my whole body shaking.

"Sir, you're going to have to leave the room."

"What's going on?"

I couldn't focus, couldn't do anything, but people were shoving me out of the room, and words like "cardiac arrest" and "coding" filtered through the haze of my brain.

It didn't make any sense.

Marley was having a baby. She was in labor and doing wonderful. What the hell was going on?

"Wait, what's going on? Somebody tell me what's going on."

"Sir, go into the waiting room with your family. We'll come give you an update soon."

I tried to move past the small woman, but then a large nurse came forward, his muscles practically bulging through his scrubs.

"Mr. Montgomery. You're going to need to come with me."

I could still hear the sounds of the monitors blaring, people moving around.

"I need to know what's happening. That's my girlfriend in there. She's having my baby. Our baby. What's wrong with Marley?"

"Sir. Please come with me."

I didn't realize I was screaming, trying to push through, until I was through the double doors and they were calling security.

And then my dad was there. I held back the bile sliding up my throat and I looked at my father, shaking.

"What's going on?" Alex Montgomery asked, looking at me, then over at the nurse.

"You're going to need to tell your son to calm down, before we'll let you know what's going on."

"I need to see Marley!" I called out, and then my mom was holding me, and my twin sister Aria took my hand.

The younger twins, Gus and Dara, held me as well. Security went away and I just stood there, waiting.

"What's going on?" my mother asked, and I looked into the eyes of Tabby Montgomery and wanted my mom to hold me and never let go.

"I don't know. Everything started beeping, and she got dizzy, and then they pushed me out. I don't know what's going on."

"I'm going to figure out what it is," Marley's dad said, rage on his face. He stormed towards the front desk, as I just tried not to throw up.

"I have power of attorney. We're not married yet. So we made sure I had power of attorney. I'm her contact. Her next of kin. The baby's next of kin. Right? Is that how it works?"

My family knew all of this, but I couldn't stop rambling.

My dad gave me a look. "Okay. Sit down, we're going to get you some water, and we're going to wait. We're just going to wait and see what they have to say."

He shared a look with my mom, one I couldn't read, one that made me want to throw up. Because the look of concern and worry sliding through his gaze, even though he tried to hide it, told me that this was bad.

So fucking bad.

Marley's father stomped away from the front desk and went straight to his wife. Marley's mom looked at me with broken eyes before she sat down and closed her eyes, her hands clasped in front of her.

My cousins and aunts and uncles and grandparents all wanted to be here, to welcome my child into the world. To be here for Marley and me, but the waiting room was small, and only one person was allowed in the room at a time.

It had been a fight for me to be in there versus Marley's mother.

But Marley wanted me in there, and we had had the paperwork to prove it.

Everything about this pregnancy had been a fight.

But not Marley. She had been perfection.

"I need her to be okay, Dad."

My dad gripped the back of my neck and pressed his forehead to mine.

"You can do this. We're here. Right here."

He didn't tell me she would be okay.

Because my dad didn't lie to me. He had his own reasons for never lying, for even trying to blunt the truth a bit to calm somebody. But he never lied to me.

I needed my dad to lie to me right then.

It felt like an hour, four, I didn't know.

But there were no updates. I just sat there, refusing to stand, as my family took turns holding me, telling me that they were there for me.

I didn't realize that tears were sliding down my cheeks until later.

We Montgomerys stuck together. We weren't going to stop.

Finally, the door opened, and I looked up at the man who had been Marley's doctor this entire time. Who had been with us when we realized we were going to be teenage parents. Adults in the eyes of the law and in our own, but not in the eyes of some of the world.

I saw the grayness on his face and I didn't want him to speak. I wanted him to walk back in there and never tell us.

Silence engulfed the room, a single pin drop would create a cacophony of sound that would change the world forever.

That would change my world forever.

"Mr. Montgomery."

"What about my daughter?" Marley's dad snapped, and the doctor looked at him, then back at me. Because this doctor knew all of the issues with Marley's parents. And knew that while I had power of attorney, they were still Marley's parents. This should have been a time of celebration and stress and happiness.

But I didn't want the doctor to speak. I couldn't.

"Mr. Montgomery. Marley went into cardiac arrest. I'm so sorry. But she's dead."

He continued to say something, about a placental abruption, about the taxing on her heart that they hadn't realized in time. A most likely genetic defect that they would talk about later.

Marley was eighteen. Soon to be nineteen.

How did an eighteen-year-old have a heart attack?

Later I would remember the screaming. That Marley's mother fell down, and nurses ran to her.

Later I would remember Marley's father screaming in my face, shoving me, and my brother and father pushing the man back, telling him to shut it down.

I would remember my mother and twin sister holding me as my baby sister began to pace, texting the family group chat, so they all knew what was going on.

In the moment I didn't know anything other than Marley was gone, but that wasn't the end of it.

I moved a step towards the doctor, ignoring the racket behind me.

"The baby?" I croaked. "Did we lose the baby?"

Had I lost my family?

Everyone went silent.

Marley was gone. How the hell had that happened? But I needed to know about the baby.

"Mr. Montgomery, your daughter is alive. She's being seen to now. Come with me."

Marley's parents began shouting again, but out of the corner of my eye, I saw my own parents holding them back. I didn't know what would happen or what we needed to do.

I didn't know what I was supposed to do.

My daughter.

We hadn't known the sex of the baby, had wanted it to be a surprise.

We had wanted today of all days to be a joyous surprise.

Not this surprise. Never this surprise.

I kept moving as I saw Leif, Nick, and Lake run into the waiting room behind me, out of breath, their eyes wide. Everyone started speaking at once, but I followed the doctor, leaving them all behind.

I didn't remember what happened next, didn't remember the route through the hallway, beyond seeing a few glances from nurses, that pitying look that made me want to vomit.

I couldn't hear anything, couldn't taste, couldn't do anything.

All I remembered was suddenly I was in a gown,

wearing gloves, hands open, arms outstretched, waiting.

The nurse came forward, a small bundle in a cream blanket in her arms, a tiny little pink hat on the baby's head.

"Mr. Montgomery, here's your daughter." She whispered a few other things about passing all her tests and the baby was healthy. About her weight and her length and the time of birth. I knew there would be paperwork later, a birth certificate to sign. All the little things that Marley and I had researched.

But what was I supposed to do now?

The nurse slid the baby into my arms, and my knees went weak. They gently settled me into a chair. I might have said thank you, but I wasn't sure.

I looked down at my daughter, our daughter, and tried to contemplate what life could be, what this moment meant.

Broken didn't begin to describe this moment. Shattered remains of who I should have been.

Our plans had been destroyed. Our path and promises to each other had been shattered.

Marley was gone. Dead. What did that word even mean?

I was nineteen years old. I wasn't supposed to be here alone.

Then I looked down at the scrunched-up little face

in my hands, at the tiny little fingers that didn't even seem real.

And I knew, I knew that I didn't have time to be selfish. Didn't have time to wonder why.

I didn't have time.

"Hi, Nora," I whispered, my voice breaking. "I'm your daddy. I'll be here. We've got this."

And then I broke down, holding my daughter, the tears flowing, and knew the world had changed.

My world had changed.

Forever.

NEXT IN THE MONTGOMERY INK LEGACY SERIES:
Sebastian finds his new path in Longtime Crush.

IF YOU'D LIKE TO READ A BONUS SCENE FROM NICK & LAKE:
CHECK OUT THIS SPECIAL EPILOGUE!

Bonus Epilogue

Nick

Montgomery dinners were something I was used to. I had been going to them since I was a teenager, though the look of them might have changed a bit over the years.

Leif and I had been scrawny teenagers, trying to figure out who we were in the world, trying to come up with insane ways to hit on people or at least gain the courage to even talk to them.

Austin and Sierra Montgomery had always been there for me. They were my rocks. Somehow that big, bearded man who looked like he could break you with his pinky had the softest heart in the world, and Sierra had the strength of a thousand moms.

I had always had a crush on Sierra, not that I had ever told Leif, though Leif had figured it out. She had giggled when we were younger but had never teased me about it.

What was I supposed to do but fall in love with my best friend's mom?

Today's dinner was in Denver this time, at Austin and Sierra's house, though only Leif was there. Their other kids were all out with various activities or living their lives.

Lake's parents had driven down from Boulder, along with her siblings, so it was our family affair.

With Liam and Arden Montgomery, Lake's siblings, Leif, Brooke, Luke, Leif's parents, and my mom.

I smiled at my mom and she grinned right back, talking to Sierra and Arden in the corner.

Mom had even brought over her own potato salad, something I hadn't had since my dad died.

When a familiar large shape sidled up next to me, I looked over at Leif and took the beer from his hand.

"Thank you."

"You're welcome. I saw you over here looking all mopey, thought I'd see what was up."

I snorted, toasted my beer with his. "I'm not mopey. Just thinking."

"I'm glad your mom is here," Leif said. I grinned at him.

"I am too. Who would've thought, right?"

"You know my birth mom. I don't think we need to start comparing, do we?"

I winced, remembering Leif's past. "Okay, fine. You win. However, you are a Montgomery, so I guess you always win."

"Did someone say Montgomery and winning?" Lake asked as she came forward. I lifted my arm and she slid right against me, as if she were a perfect fit.

As if she should have been here the whole time.

I still couldn't quite believe it.

"So, what did I miss?" she asked. I leaned down and brushed my lips against hers.

She moaned against me, smiling softly, as Leif cleared his throat.

"That's my almost sister there. Watch it, buddy."

Lake snarled. "Almost sister? Cousin, thank you very much. Let's not get too banjo here."

"Stop knocking the banjo," Brooke said with a laugh as she handed Luke a napkin. He wiped his little face, and I shook my head, smiling at the kid. He had every single person here wrapped around his finger, and I just grinned.

"Your parents sure do love being grandparents, even though it's not official yet."

"It will be soon. Hey, we have two weddings coming up. Maybe we should just do them together and get it over with," Leif said quickly.

Brooke's head shot up as I whistled through my teeth and Lake started laughing.

"Did you just say 'get it over with' for a wedding?" the love of my life asked as I held back laughter.

"No, we want two weddings," Lake's mom put in. "Because you two are completely different couples, and this way this little guy can be the ring bearer twice."

"I get to be the ring man."

I frowned and looked at Leif.

"Well, you're my best man, just like I'm yours, but Luke is sort of going to fill that role too. And my ring bearer. I mean, why not?"

"The ring man. I like it," I said as Luke came up to me, and I lifted him up onto my hip.

"So I take it you're our ring bearer."

"Well, you haven't asked," Luke said with an exaggerated sigh, and I held back a smile as everybody laughed.

"Okay, Lake, should we ask?"

"I don't know. Maybe I should see if my brother Anton wants to do it."

Luke's eyes widened. "Anton is like an adult now. It should totally be me."

I held back a smile. "Fourteen isn't quite an adult, but you never know."

"I don't know how we will fit everybody on both sides of the aisle. Especially with so many Montgomerys," Brooke put in.

"And you know, we do have friends outside of the family," Lake added.

"You do?" Leif and I said at the same time before we clinked our beers, and all of our parents laughed.

"What we did was take turns," Austin put in. "So we just decided who would be best man and sort of worked it around in a circle. Ish. All that matters is you have people who want to stand up for you. That love you. Everything else is just cake."

"There'll be cake?" Luke asked, and I smiled.

"Oh yes, we're going to have cake. And there's going to be a groom's cake, right? I get a cake of my own?"

"If you want cake, we can get you cake," Lake said, as she kissed me.

Luke pushed me away and went to kiss Lake on her cheek, and she fluttered her lashes.

"Well then. Thank you, Luke."

"Well, if you're not going to marry me, who will?"

Jemma, Lake's sister, came forward, the sixteen-year-old, all limbs, laughed, and plucked Luke up from my arms.

"I guess it's me. But I think we're going to be family now. Maybe cousins?"

"Let's not discuss the family tree. It gets confusing," Lake said, and I snorted.

"Just a little. Either way, I guess we're planning weddings. How the hell did that happen?"

"Language," nearly everyone said in the room at once, including Luke.

I rolled my eyes, kissed Lake hard on the mouth, and knew I was right where I needed to be.

"As long as there's cake, a wedding's fine."

"I'm sure we can think of something that's better than just cake."

"I don't know. Cake is the best."

"And now I want cake," Leif grumbled beside me.

I shook my head, hugged Lake close, and looked around the family that I had made.

I might not be a Montgomery by birth, but I was one anyway.

Because once they grabbed onto you, they never let go.

And with Lake in my arms? I didn't mind one bit.

NEXT IN THE MONTGOMERY INK LEGACY SERIES:
Sebastian finds his new path in Longtime Crush.

A Note from Carrie
Ann Ryan

Thank you so much for reading **AT FIRST MEET.**

Going back to the origins of the Montgomerys was like going back in time and yet flinging myself into the future all at once.

I met Lake in a free story I wrote for an anthology called Inked Fantasy. I knew she was this spunky kid who had wonderful parents and could fight the world.

When she showed up in the Montgomery Ink Legacy series as I was plotting, she was the GIRL BOSS I always wanted to be.

So her HEA needed to be with a gruff, angry... totally a marshmallow guy. Enter her friend and enemy: Nick.

This story wasn't easy to write. Lake's journey was something very personal to me. Something I knew that

I needed to write because of my own journey from before I was married.

And that is why Lake could show the strength she had throughout this book.

And why I love Nick.

If you'd like May's book, her romance with Leo is Happily Ever Never!

Next up is Sebastian.

I love him. I've loved him since I met him as a wee baby in the Montgomery Ink series. His parents' book is my one of my favorites ever.

And I knew what needed to happen before I wrote the first book.

So, yes, this book is hard. But he will find his happiness.

And thank you for reading the Montgomerys. They love you.

As do I.

The Montgomery Ink Legacy Series:
Book 1: Bittersweet Promises
Book 2: At First Meet
Book 2.5: Happily Ever Never
Book 3: Longtime Crush
Book 4: Best Friend Temptation

IF YOU'D LIKE TO READ A BONUS SCENE FROM NICK & LAKE:
CHECK OUT THIS SPECIAL EPILOGUE!

NEXT IN THE MONTGOMERY INK LEGACY SERIES:
Sebastian finds his new path in Longtime Crush.

If you want to make sure you know what's coming next from me, you can sign up for my newsletter at www. CarrieAnnRyan.com; follow me on twitter at @CarrieAnnRyan, or like my Facebook page. I also have a Facebook Fan Club where we have trivia, chats, and other goodies. You guys are the reason I get to do what I do and I thank you.

Make sure you're signed up for my MAILING LIST so you can know when the next releases are available as well as find giveaways and FREE READS.

Happy Reading!

Also from Carrie Ann Ryan

The Montgomery Ink Legacy Series:
Book 1: Bittersweet Promises
Book 2: At First Meet
Book 2.5: Happily Ever Never
Book 3: Longtime Crush
Book 4: Best Friend Temptation

The Wilder Brothers Series:
Book 1: One Way Back to Me
Book 2: Always the One for Me
Book 3: The Path to You
Book 4: Coming Home for Us
Book 5: Stay Here With Me

The Aspen Pack Series:

Book 1: Etched in Honor

Book 2: Hunted in Darkness

Book 3: Mated in Chaos

Book 4: Harbored in Silence

Book 5: Marked in Flames

The Montgomery Ink: Fort Collins Series:

Book 1: Inked Persuasion

Book 2: Inked Obsession

Book 3: Inked Devotion

Book 3.5: Nothing But Ink

Book 4: Inked Craving

Book 5: Inked Temptation

The Montgomery Ink: Boulder Series:

Book 1: Wrapped in Ink

Book 2: Sated in Ink

Book 3: Embraced in Ink

Book 3: Moments in Ink

Book 4: Seduced in Ink

Book 4.5: Captured in Ink

Book 4.7: Inked Fantasy

Book 4.8: A Very Montgomery Christmas

Montgomery Ink: Colorado Springs

Book 1: Fallen Ink

Book 2: Restless Ink

Book 2.5: Ashes to Ink
Book 3: Jagged Ink
Book 3.5: Ink by Numbers

Montgomery Ink Denver:
Book 0.5: Ink Inspired
Book 0.6: Ink Reunited
Book 1: Delicate Ink
Book 1.5: Forever Ink
Book 2: Tempting Boundaries
Book 3: Harder than Words
Book 3.5: Finally Found You
Book 4: Written in Ink
Book 4.5: Hidden Ink
Book 5: Ink Enduring
Book 6: Ink Exposed
Book 6.5: Adoring Ink
Book 6.6: Love, Honor, & Ink
Book 7: Inked Expressions
Book 7.3: Dropout
Book 7.5: Executive Ink
Book 8: Inked Memories
Book 8.5: Inked Nights
Book 8.7: Second Chance Ink
Book 8.5: Montgomery Midnight Kisses
Bonus: Inked Kingdom

Also from Carrie Ann Ryan

The On My Own Series:
Book 0.5: My First Glance
Book 1: My One Night
Book 2: My Rebound
Book 3: My Next Play
Book 4: My Bad Decisions

The Promise Me Series:
Book 1: Forever Only Once
Book 2: From That Moment
Book 3: Far From Destined
Book 4: From Our First

The Less Than Series:
Book 1: Breathless With Her
Book 2: Reckless With You
Book 3: Shameless With Him

The Fractured Connections Series:
Book 1: Breaking Without You
Book 2: Shouldn't Have You
Book 3: Falling With You
Book 4: Taken With You

The Whiskey and Lies Series:
Book 1: Whiskey Secrets
Book 2: Whiskey Reveals

Book 3: Whiskey Undone

The Gallagher Brothers Series:
Book 1: Love Restored
Book 2: Passion Restored
Book 3: Hope Restored

The Ravenwood Coven Series:
Book 1: Dawn Unearthed
Book 2: Dusk Unveiled
Book 3: Evernight Unleashed

The Talon Pack:
Book 1: Tattered Loyalties
Book 2: An Alpha's Choice
Book 3: Mated in Mist
Book 4: Wolf Betrayed
Book 5: Fractured Silence
Book 6: Destiny Disgraced
Book 7: Eternal Mourning
Book 8: Strength Enduring
Book 9: Forever Broken
Book 10: Mated in Darkness
Book 11: Fated in Winter

Redwood Pack Series:
Book 1: An Alpha's Path

Book 2: A Taste for a Mate
Book 3: Trinity Bound
Book 3.5: A Night Away
Book 4: Enforcer's Redemption
Book 4.5: Blurred Expectations
Book 4.7: Forgiveness
Book 5: Shattered Emotions
Book 6: Hidden Destiny
Book 6.5: A Beta's Haven
Book 7: Fighting Fate
Book 7.5: Loving the Omega
Book 7.7: The Hunted Heart
Book 8: Wicked Wolf

The Elements of Five Series:

Book 1: From Breath and Ruin
Book 2: From Flame and Ash
Book 3: From Spirit and Binding
Book 4: From Shadow and Silence

Dante's Circle Series:

Book 1: Dust of My Wings
Book 2: Her Warriors' Three Wishes
Book 3: An Unlucky Moon
Book 3.5: His Choice
Book 4: Tangled Innocence
Book 5: Fierce Enchantment

Book 6: <u>An Immortal's Song</u>
Book 7: <u>Prowled Darkness</u>
Book 8: Dante's Circle Reborn

Holiday, Montana Series:
Book 1: <u>Charmed Spirits</u>
Book 2: <u>Santa's Executive</u>
Book 3: <u>Finding Abigail</u>
Book 4: <u>Her Lucky Love</u>
Book 5: Dreams of Ivory

The Branded Pack Series:
(Written with Alexandra Ivy)
Book 1: <u>Stolen and Forgiven</u>
Book 2: <u>Abandoned and Unseen</u>
Book 3: <u>Buried and Shadowed</u>

About the Author

Carrie Ann Ryan is the New York Times and USA Today bestselling author of contemporary, paranormal, and young adult romance. Her works include the Montgomery Ink, Redwood Pack, Fractured Connections, and Elements of Five series, which have sold over 3.0 million books worldwide. She started writing while in graduate school for her advanced degree in chemistry and hasn't stopped since. Carrie Ann has written over seventy-five novels and novellas with more in the works. When she's not losing herself in her emotional and action-packed worlds, she's reading as much as she can while wrangling her clowder of cats who have more followers than she does.

www.CarrieAnnRyan.com

www.ingramcontent.com/pod-product-compliance
Lightning Source LLC
Chambersburg PA
CBHW010735130726
47899CB00015B/3269

* 9 7 8 1 6 3 6 9 5 1 8 2 9 *